THE
LION HUNTER

THE LION HUNTER

THE MARK OF SOLOMON ~ BOOK ONE

ELIZABETH E. WEIN

VIKING

VIKING
Published by Penguin Group
Penguin Group (USA) Inc., 345 Hudson Street, New York, New York 10014, U.S.A.
Penguin Group (Canada), 90 Eglinton Avenue East, Suite 700, Toronto, Ontario, Canada M4P 2Y3
(a division of Pearson Penguin Canada Inc.)
Penguin Books Ltd, 80 Strand, London WC2R 0RL, England
Penguin Ireland, 25 St Stephen's Green, Dublin 2, Ireland (a division of Penguin Books Ltd)
Penguin Group (Australia), 250 Camberwell Road, Camberwell, Victoria 3124, Australia
(a division of Pearson Australia Group Pty Ltd)
Penguin Books India Pvt Ltd, 11 Community Centre, Panchsheel Park, New Delhi—110 017, India
Penguin Group (NZ), 67 Apollo Drive, Mairangi Bay, Auckland 1311, New Zealand
Penguin Books (South Africa) (Pty) Ltd, 24 Sturdee Avenue, Rosebank, Johannesburg 2196, South Africa

Penguin Books Ltd, Registered Offices: 80 Strand, London WC2R 0RL, England

First published in 2007 by Viking, a member of Penguin Group (USA) Inc.

3   5   7   9   10   8   6   4   2

Copyright © Elizabeth Gatland, 2007

LIBRARY OF CONGRESS CATALOGING-IN-PUBLICATION DATA IS AVAILABLE
ISBN 978-0-670-06163-1

Printed in U.S.A.
Set in Goudy Old Style
Book design by Jim Hoover

The publisher does not have any control over and does not assume any responsibility
for author or third-party Web sites or their content.

For Mark

Contents

I. BLIND TRUST 1

II. IMAGINARY BEASTS 14

III. ATHENA 25

IV. THE LURE OF SHADOWS 40

V. LOAVES AND FISHES 50

VI. HOPE 63

VII. THE GATES THROWN WIDE 81

VIII. A SHOUT IN THE STREET 94

IX. THE HANISH ISLANDS 108

X. THE HANGED MAN 120

XI. STAIRWAYS 139

XII. STAR MASTER AND MORNINGSTAR 157

XIII. TAMING THE LION 176

XIV. THE COVENANT 199

AUTHOR'S NOTE 218

GLOSSARY 222

FAMILY TREE 224

THE ARABIAN PENINSULA

100 miles

PERSIAN GULF

RED SEA

NIZAR

GHASSAN

KINDA

MA'IN

EMPTY QUARTER (desert)

SHEBA

HADRAMAWT

Mecca

al-Surat Mountains

Turtle Islands

Hanish Archipelago

Marib

San'a

Zafar

QATABAN

AWSAN

Qana

Adulis

Kolöe

Adwa

Aksum

Takeze River

Simien Mountains

Debra Damo

Salt Desert

Deire

HIMYAR

al-Muza

Hot Lands

Aden

ARABIAN SEA

SOQOTRA

AFAR

Great Valley

Gulf of Aden

INDIAN OCEAN

AFRICA

Blue Nile River

"He prowled among the lions;

he became a young lion,

and he learned to catch prey...."

~EZEKIEL 19:6

I

BLIND TRUST

THE HARSH CRIES of his mother's birth pains were too heartrending for Telemakos to bear, and he had fled the house.

He spent the morning in the lion pit at the New Palace with Solomon and Sheba. Telemakos had caught the emperor's lions himself, as cubs, six years ago. He had no responsibility for them; Nezana, the royal lion keeper, saw to that. But they knew Telemakos better than anyone, and he loved them.

Today the great gold-and-black-pelted male, Solomon, was restless too, which was unlike him. Telemakos thought the lion must have picked up his mood. Usually Solomon never did anything but sleep, though on a good day he would indulge Telemakos like a cub; he would let Telemakos sit astride his back and cling to his mane as he loped gently around the pit's perimeter, or would chase colored wooden balls through the sand, retrieving them and dropping them at Telemakos's feet like a dog. Today Solomon would not stay still from one half minute to the next. This was frustrating, because Telemakos wanted comfort. Sheba was always an aloof and independent creature and would tolerate attention only a little at a time, but Telemakos counted on lazy, doggish Solomon to return his affection.

Telemakos wandered away from his disloyal friend, unconsoled. He leaped lightly onto the first of the stepping-stones that wound across the lions' trout pool. Telemakos often practiced here a small, private challenge to himself. He stood for a moment breathing carefully and finding his balance, and then he shut his eyes. He could walk the whole trail now, without looking, but he could not yet do it without faltering. The minor perils of tame lions and missed footing were distractions from his real fear, which was of covering his eyes.

It was more than half a year since he had been freed from the salt smugglers who had held him in slavery all last summer, but after having his eyes taped shut for two exhausting, appalling months, he still had a horror of being blinded. It was a trial of courage for him to pull his shirt over his head in the morning; the touch of the soft cotton on his face made his skin crawl. He had to dress and undress with his eyes and teeth clenched shut. It was such a little thing that he was ashamed to speak of it.

So he practiced covering his eyes. He could negotiate the stone path in the lions' fish pool with his eyes closed, and when his balance was perfect, he was planning to attempt it with a length of his shamma shawl pulled across his face.

But not today. Today he could not concentrate on his feet. He kept thinking about his mother, and the baby. He missed his step twice, and the second time he ended in water to his knees. Trout leaped and fled from him among the reeds and pebbles, and the lions came padding over to see what was going on.

Solomon paced at the water's edge, chirruping queries at Telemakos.

"Never mind the stepping-stones today," Telemakos said, talking aloud to set Solomon at ease.

He sloshed his way across the pool and tried to tickle Solomon behind the ears. The lion sniffed disdainfully at Telemakos's wet feet, shook himself free of Telemakos's hands, and went back to his pacing.

Telemakos sat down among the reeds at the water's edge, his toes in the shallows and his knees drawn up under his chin. I'm too excited, he thought. Solomon won't calm down as long as I keep splashing about and making the fish jump. And pretty soon Sheba will catch it, too, and then she'll snap at me.

He knew he ought to go somewhere else. He hated it when Sheba began snarling. Once, he had had to face her down until Nezana arrived with his whip and distracted the lioness long enough for Telemakos to escape up the keeper's rope.

They're *lions*, Telemakos reminded himself. They're tame and overfed, but they're lions. They just do what lions do. They can't help it.

He drew his feet back from the edge of the pool and watched the water shrinking from his skin as it dried. His feet were golden-brown, soft-hued as old honey, something in between his dark African mother's and his fair British father's. Telemakos wondered if the baby would be like him, a strange crossing of cultures, with skin the color of cinnamon and hair the color of salt. His heart leaped with pleasure and apprehension when he thought of the baby. Girl or boy? Girl, I know it. She will be a girl, and they will name her—

"Hail below!"

Telemakos looked up. His father and the keeper stood side by side, leaning over the wall where the rope was.

"Is my sister here?" Telemakos demanded, scrambling to his feet.

Nezana and Medraut laughed.

"Yes, O child oracle, your sister's here," Medraut called down. "Come home to the house of Nebir and meet her."

In his delight and excitement, Telemakos made the mistake of his life.

With the emperor's restless lions at his back, he ran toward the wall where his father stood.

"*Telemakos!*" Medraut bellowed in anguished horror, and Nezana cried out, "*Beware!*"

Telemakos had time to turn his head, and to glance behind him over his left shoulder.

Solomon, *Solomon,* lazy, gentle Solomon, had seen in Telemakos's sudden flight the moment he had dreamed of all through his narrow, pampered existence: a small, sweet-smelling, slender-legged animal racing away from him, calling

him to hunt. It did not matter that he was not hungry. It did
not occur to Solomon, in that moment of wild instinct, that
the creature fleeing across the lion pit was the same creature
that brushed his mane and rode on his back. Solomon crossed
the pit in three long, low leaps.

"Solomon! *Back!*" Telemakos shouted, and was daring and
desperate enough that he tried to turn and shout his vain command in Solomon's face. But Solomon only gave him time for
that first glance, and for Telemakos to throw his arm up and try
to shield his neck. Solomon was sevenfold Telemakos's weight.
Telemakos went down beneath him like a stem of barley to the
blade of a scythe, his hand clutching frantically at the back of
his neck, his arm bent double and trapped, nearly from wrist to
shoulder, in the brutal, saw-toothed vise of Solomon's jaws.

For what seemed a very long time, Telemakos thought
about nothing but protecting his neck.

Then his father was bundling him into his arms and weeping as he ran, and Nezana was rounding on Solomon with his
whip to hold him at bay while Medraut carried Telemakos out
through the tunnel. The jolting of his father's strides tore his
equilibrium apart, and Telemakos was sick all down Medraut's
shirt and then again all over his own arm when Medraut laid
him on the paving stones of the court outside the lion pit's
lower walls.

"You monstrous, thankless child!" his father wept. "Give
me half a chance to put you back together before you go about
polluting yourself!"

The keeper came running out to them. Medraut held on to Telemakos with iron fingers that bit into his arm more pressingly, it seemed, than Solomon's teeth had.

"Get me the emperor's physician," Medraut ordered. "And at least two attendants. A brazier, searing irons, a full kettle of clean water. Spirit, salt, a bolt of cotton, and needles, and a spool of fine gut. Opium. Now. Bring all of it out here, now. If I let go of him, he'll bleed to death."

Oh, Telemakos thought.

He lay quietly and stared at the sky, waiting for what would happen next.

Medraut bent over him as they waited, his fingers cutting into Telemakos's arm like knives. "Telemakos? *Stay here.*"

"*I am here,*" Telemakos whispered. He tried to focus on his father's face and the silver-fair hair that was like a reflection of his own, but the sky pulled back his gaze. It was the beginning of the season of the Long Rains, and though it was not raining yet that day, the air was thick with mist. The far winter sky soothed him, bright and gray and soft.

Desperate for time, they burned shut the wounds that were killing him even before they gave him the opium. No matter what they did to him, his vision never went entirely black, his mind never entirely unaware, until his inability to lose consciousness and shut it all out made him want to scream and scream and scream, except that he had no strength to do anything but stare dazedly at the sky.

His father and another man worked over his arm and shoulder with needle and thread. It was like being eaten alive by a flock of tiny birds. Something occurred to Telemakos suddenly, and he spoke through his father's endless, endless stitches.

"Oh, please—sir," Telemakos gasped. "Solomon! *Please* . . . Don't—kill—Solomon!"

"Hush, child," Medraut murmured at his ear, never hesitating in his work. "Foolish one. Would that punish Solomon, or you? The emperor won't allow his pets to be executed."

Telemakos said clearly and abruptly, "Because when she is bigger, I want to show the baby."

"Oh." Then for the first time, Medraut faltered. "The *baby!*"

Telemakos saw that his father had utterly forgotten her.

Medraut bent his head over his son. His hot tears scorched Telemakos's arm. "Better she had never been born," Medraut whispered.

After a time, with great reluctance, Telemakos realized it was easier to lie with his eyes shut than with them open.

But he stayed awake. For hours he remained aware of all that was happening to him, and dimly aware of all that was happening around him.

Gebre Meskal, the young emperor of the African kingdom of Aksum, had on several occasions let it be known publicly that he was indebted to the house of Nebir. He gave up a suite of rooms in his palace so that Telemakos would not have to be carried home in his drugged and blood-dazed stupor. Long past dark, long after there was nothing more his father could do for him, Telemakos lay conscious of Medraut kneeling with his head on the cot by his shoulder, watching the shallow rise and fall of Telemakos's chest as he breathed.

It seemed late at night when the emperor came in.

"Ras Meder."

Gebre Meskal used Medraut's Ethiopic name and royal title, Prince Meder, as Telemakos did when he addressed his father. Telemakos felt his father come to attention.

"Majesty."

"Be at ease, sir," said the emperor, and sighed. "Please. Take my hand. Sit. Never have I known a birthday smutted by a grimmer cloud. Will he heal?"

Medraut's answer was no answer. "He bore our surgery like a soldier."

"So he would. His mettle bests the better part of my army. Telemakos Lionheart, Beloved Telemakos. Few men could have endured the punishment he suffered in the hands of the smugglers at the Afar mines, when he sought to discover those who would sabotage my plague quarantine. And he was only a child."

In gentle affection, the emperor brushed his cool, dry palm over Telemakos's forehead.

"Beloved Telemakos," he repeated.

Even so innocent a touch, so close to Telemakos's eyes, made him shudder. For one endless, confusing moment, Telemakos thought he was there, back in Afar. The brutal foreman that he never saw was tightening the blindfold—Telemakos was lost again in a dark, constricted world of thirst and exhaustion, labor and torment, where his eyes were always covered and his arms always bound, and his legs were locked in iron while he slept. If he lay blind and unable to move like this, where else could he be but in Afar, in the Salt Desert?

But, but. The emperor was still talking.

"—he was only a child. What age is he now?"

Medraut answered with dull, mechanical politeness. "He will be twelve at Trinity next month."

"I have kept my eye on your lionhearted son this past half year," the emperor said in a low voice. "I would not use so young a servant as a spy another time. It was a season before he had his full weight back after the captivity. And I have lain awake some nights regretting how publicly I involved him in the trial that followed. I should not have risked bringing anyone's wrath against the boy."

Medraut let out a sharp breath of dismissal. "Wrath!" he said hoarsely, his voice rough with unhappiness. "Majesty, what does any of that matter now? What more evil could be done to him than this? If any one of these wounds should fester, only one . . . Tooth and claw. There are so many. I dread their infection."

"It is past curfew, Ras Meder," the emperor said quietly. "I am holding the Guardian's Gate open for you. I want you to go home."

Medraut let one hand fall on Telemakos's chest, and

Telemakos gasped faintly. His torn ribcage throbbed beneath the pressure of his father's touch, but it was a relief to feel its firm reality. He was not in Afar.

"I myself will keep your watch this night," said Gebre Meskal. "You, Ras Meder, have the boy's grieving mother and newborn sister waiting for your comfort. Your son is at rest for the moment. Please go home now."

There were not many who could command Telemakos's father, Medraut the son of Artos the Dragon, Medraut who would now be high king of Britain if he had so desired. "I should do this for no other man," Medraut said in a low voice, rising to his feet.

"Do it for no man's sake. Do it for Turunesh your wife, and your new daughter. Ras Meder—"

The emperor spoke steadily. "Ras Meder, I have a question to put to you before you go. Let me ask it quickly, for I do not like to consult you on matters of policy when you are so pressed with hope and fear for your children. But it cannot wait. A dispatch has come this morning, and I must send an answer before rain makes the roads impassable. My cousin the king of Himyar, Abreha Anbessa, whom the Himyarites name Lion Hunter, wants me to lift my quarantine."

Telemakos's mind went suddenly keen, clutching at this distraction. Even only half-conscious, he was fascinated as always by the complicated adult world of power and influence that surrounded him.

"Why do you consult me?" Medraut said. "Consult my sister, the princess Goewin, your so-called British *ambassador*. She is your Mentor, not I; your Athena, your queen of spies."

"Do not ever call her that," the emperor said sharply, "even though we are alone."

"Your pardon, sir," Medraut muttered. "But why consult me?"

"Because you are a doctor. I want to know what risk I run of bringing plague to Aksum if I lift my quarantine and resume trade in the Red Sea. Abreha has his eye fixed on the Hanish Islands, and I fear he will try to secure them if I do not exercise my right of dominion there. He has been my ally these six years, and I do not want to wake the ghost of my father's conflict in Arabia."

Oh, the wealth of intrigue you heard when no one imagined you were listening.

Telemakos tried to divest himself of his ruined arm and the numbing, flashed return to last summer's captivity, to concentrate on the low voices over his head.

"What do you lose if you lose Hanish?" Medraut asked.

"A colony of exile and our first port of entry from the Orient to the Red Sea, since plague took Deire. A vast mine of obsidian. Rich pearl-fishing grounds."

"Majesty, run the risk of losing Hanish. Have you condemned whole cities and plunged nobles into poverty with your quarantine, to be tempted by a handful of obsidian and pearls? Throw wide your gates before time, and your people will fall to plague like corn to locusts; they will have no hardiness against a disease they have scarcely encountered."

Medraut drew a long breath. But he finished firmly, "Ask that your cousin forgive you for refusing his request. Abreha Anbessa is a forgiving man. Show him that you trust him. Hold your quarantine another year."

It took every fragment of Telemakos's will to understand and remember this exchange.

"So. The quarantine holds. Thank you, Ras Meder."

"It is advice easily given. It is not so easily enforced."

"The quarantine holds."

This assertion seemed curiously reassuring. Telemakos opened his eyes.

"You prying young demon. You never miss a word." Medraut drummed his fingers against Telemakos's chest, his touch fond and feather light, so that Telemakos hardly felt it. "Look at this, my lord, he is awake. He is hanging on our every syllable."

Medraut bent near him, searching his face. Telemakos watched but could not move his head.

"Queen?"

Telemakos made the word with tongue and teeth, but no sound came out. With a great effort, he gathered himself.

"Queen of spies?" he whispered.

His father and Gebre Meskal glanced at each other over Telemakos's still form. Then the emperor leaned close to him as well, with one finger raised to his own lips.

"It is a secret," he said. "No man must ever know the true name of my Mentor"—his voice was gentle—"or that of my sunbird."

That had been Gebre Meskal's name for Telemakos him-self, when Telemakos had moved in listening secrecy, alone in Afar among the salt pirates, the year before.

But no one knows my name, Telemakos thought. Our ports are closed, the black market was stopped six months ago, the men who ran it are all exiled or dead. Why then, he thought, and this time found himself shaping words without meaning to: "Why now, if all is finished—?"

It was utterly exhausting to try to speak aloud. Telemakos closed his eyes again.

"All is not finished," said the emperor Gebre Meskal.

II

IMAGINARY BEASTS

TELEMAKOS LAY IN the New Palace for a month. A day or so after the accident, when he was vaguely sensible again, he begged so piteously to go home that they finally sent for his aunt to come stay with him. It was not the same as being at home, sharing an apartment with Goewin in the New Palace, but it was a little like last year's arrangement in the governor's house at Adulis, when Telemakos had first begun to uncover the plot to undermine Gebre Meskal's quarantine. Goewin came to sit on the edge of Telemakos's bed after her day's meetings were finished, just as she had done in Adulis. She read to him from Homer's *Odyssey*, his favorite book.

"Do you think Telemakos knows?" Telemakos asked about his namesake, Odysseus's son. He had to whisper because he could not talk. "Do you think he knows that Mentor is really Athena—his advisor is the goddess Athena, inspiring him to do everything he does?"

"Of course he knows."

"He always pretends he doesn't."

"He is a diplomat. Prudent Telemakos," Goewin said, turning and settling the pages. "Athena likes to hide her nature. The advisor Mentor is only a mortal, a loyal servant of the king. He has no special power to speak of, other than wisdom. It is the perfect disguise for the goddess."

"You are my Mentor," Telemakos whispered.

Goewin looked up sharply. If Telemakos had not loved her as much as he did, he would have been afraid of her warning glare; she was so different from everyone else, black haired and white faced, tall and pale and proud.

"I see why you would call me that," she said. "We've always been like that. The first thing you ever said to me was to quote Telemakos's welcome to the goddess."

Goewin put aside the manuscript pages and laid one cool hand on his forehead, to smooth the pale hair back from his brown skin.

"But Telemakos, there is a reason you ought not to call me Mentor."

"I know. I heard—" Telemakos hesitated. He had tensed at her touch. She had seen it and, perhaps thinking it hurt him, took her hand away. "Ras Meder and Gebre Meskal were talking about you," Telemakos said. "They called you Gebre Meskal's Mentor. 'Queen of spies,' they called you."

"You should know," Goewin agreed. "But it is knowledge worth as much as my life. Or yours, should an evil mind make the connection. Don't speak it aloud carelessly, even when we are alone."

They were nearly the emperor's exact words. And it could scarcely be said that Telemakos had spoken aloud.

Goewin sat back and picked up the book again. She took a breath as if she was about to continue reading, but Telemakos stopped her.

"Goewin," he whispered, "have you been threatened again?"

"I am threatened daily," she said, as if it were nothing.

No one had liked the quarantine when it first began, and people blamed it on Goewin because, in her role as the British ambassador, she had first suggested it. There were ugly messages pinned to Grandfather's gate with knives, and the skull of a lioness with an arrow wired through it, and once, a sinisterly mutilated doll carved in salt, white faced and bloodied.

"You get threats because of the quarantine. Because you are Goewin. But you are also . . . You captain those who serve the emperor in secret. And someone knows?"

"They don't know anything," Goewin answered contemptuously. "Someone is trying to frighten us, but they are not doing a very good job. They have to use their own code words. Old ones. They still call me hyena, as they called you harrier, once, having no other idea of what I am. So—a hyena's head arrives in the emperor's kitchens one day, hidden in a crate of coconuts. And similar clever tricks. Some pirate we didn't catch is growing bored, with no salt shipments to arrange, all his friends in exile and no one to talk to."

Goewin looked up from the book and saw Telemakos frowning at her in calculating concentration.

"There's no connection between the murdered lioness sent to our house and the murdered hyena sent to this palace," she said more calmly. "There's no connection between Goewin and Mentor. Some threats are openly aimed at me. These are not. Oh—"

"At me, then?" Telemakos croaked. "At the sunbird? Don't tell me, I have it. Not at the sunbird, but at the harrier! That's what they called me, isn't it? Have they found dead harriers in among the royal chickens?"

Goewin let out a bark of laughter. Telemakos found himself choking on painful laughter as well.

"You are terrible, boy. It's not a joke."

"They have! Someone kills harriers and sends them to Gebre Meskal!" It was tremendous that Telemakos should be lying here, half-dead, and out in the streets of Aksum some-one imagined his secret self to be dangerous and frightening enough to warrant sending threats to the emperor.

Goewin nodded.

"But they don't know it's me," Telemakos said firmly.

"They do not. But I don't like it. It means there's someone we haven't accounted for. . . ."

Goewin slapped the book down on the floor. She stood and walked to the window, where she put up both hands to rattle them among the colored glass beads and strips of beaten copper that she had hung there to catch the light. "Let's talk of something else, Telemakos."

"Tell me about my sister," he demanded immediately.

Goewin smiled. She stood with her back to the window, one hand still playing lightly among the wind chimes. "I will bring her to see you someday soon," Goewin said. "If your father allows you company. She's fussier than you, though. She cries and cries and cries. The only time she ever stops is when she's suckling, or sleeping on top of someone."

"Does she sleep on top of you?"

"I took her to bed with me for two nights, just after she was born," Goewin said. "Otherwise your mother would never have got any sleep at all. Then I came here, of course."

"If Ras Meder would let me go home, the baby could sleep on me," Telemakos suggested.

Goewin gave him a withering look. "Do you think your father will allow a wriggling slug of a baby kicking at your bare ribs anytime soon, boy? Maybe after your skin grows back."

His ribs and throat and shoulder slowly began to heal. His arm began to rot.

Two weeks after the accident, they drugged him utterly senseless for half a day so that they could cut out the pieces of him that were going moldy. After that he was so pathetic for a few days that he was able only to sip broth fed to him by Goewin in endless, patient spoonfuls. But by the end of the month he could feed himself, and he went four whole days without running a fever.

"I am minded to allow you visitors," his father said. "Your friend Sofya has been battering at your door for the last three weeks, trying to get past me. Would you like to see Sofya?"

"I want to go home," Telemakos said.

At the end of the week his father was so tired of listening to his pleading that at last they took him back to his own bedroom.

They made him endure another three days of proving he was not at risk of fever before they brought his baby sister in to him for five minutes. She was asleep. Their mother, Turunesh, stood just inside Telemakos's bedroom door with the baby snuggled tightly over her stomach in a wide swathe of fabric. Telemakos could see nothing of his sister but the top of her head, a startling shock of loose, shining bronze curls. He could not see her, but while Turunesh stood there, he could smell her: an unfamiliar baby smell, of new milk turning sour, and starch, and herb-scented oil, and sandalwood.

"I'm sorry you can't see her face, my love," Turunesh said. "All is misery when she's awake."

They had not given her a name yet.

"She smells good," Telemakos said. "What will we call her?"

His mother rubbed her eyes with the back of one hand. "I don't know. We haven't talked about it. We haven't had a chance to talk." She turned to go out, and said over her shoulder, "I'll see if Goewin will take her. Then I can come back and sit with you awhile."

"Just sit anyway," Telemakos said. "The baby can't bother me when she's *asleep*."

"She'll wake up if I sit," Turunesh said. "And then none of us will have any peace till evening."

They let him have other brief glimpses of the baby over the next week, but they never let her get close to him, and he never saw her with her eyes open. Then one night he woke up feeling hot and sick, and he could smell the decay starting in his arm again. After that there were no more visits from the baby. Medraut and the emperor's physician, Amosi, spent most of a day repeating the operation of a month ago, until there was so little left of Telemakos's arm it made him sick to his stomach to look at it.

Amosi came back two days later to examine the wounds, and thinking Telemakos to be insensible because his eyes were closed, said frankly to Telemakos's father: "Look at this—half his shoulder gone, bone laid bare! This will be septic again before the week is out. You are making your half-grown son endure torture I would not inflict on a grown man! With each effort to save his arm, you risk stopping his heart. Take the arm off and be done with it!"

"I will not," Medraut answered, his voice tight with fury and worry. "I *will not* take his arm off."

◆   ◆   ◆

After the second operation, Telemakos began to have nightmares. He woke up screaming more often than the baby did. Medraut took to spending every third or fourth night in the monastery above the city because it was the only way he could stay alert enough to give Telemakos the attention he needed.

Telemakos screamed himself awake in the middle of one night.

"Do not, *do not*, oh, SAVE ME!"

He opened his eyes in panic. Even awake he could not move.

Goewin was sitting beside him. There was a blue-and-white ceramic oil lamp on the floor at her feet and a shamma shawl over her lap, as if she had already been there for some time.

"So, so, so," she murmured soothingly, and rocked back and forth in her chair, but she did not reach to touch him. "Telemakos," she said, her voice full of unhappiness, "tell me what you dream, my love."

He lay sobbing and did not answer.

"Sometimes if you tell a bad dream aloud, it doesn't seem so terrible," she said, still rocking her knees gently to and fro. "Your father used to write his down. He spent an entire winter chronicling his nightmares, just before our father's estate at Camlan was destroyed, and he let me read them, too."

In his sleep, Telemakos had thought himself surrounded by the baboonlike stench of Anako the salt smuggler, and it bewildered him, on waking, to find the air full of sandalwood.

"All right," Telemakos whispered, ready to try anything.

"All right. It's the men in Afar. At the salt mines last summer, when the smugglers caught me, I pretended I was mute. They thought I must be hiding something, so they tried to make me scream, to see if I could talk. That part was real."

Goewin closed her eyes, her knees swaying. Telemakos had never given her much detail about what had happened to him in Afar.

"In the dream they know I can talk, and they want to know who sent me. That's all he asks, Anako, the ringleader, again and again: *Who sent you?* And I mustn't answer. And every time he asks and I don't answer, he tells the other one, the warden at the salt mines, to drive a nail through my arm with a hammer. And he does. And—"

The fever made Telemakos feel as though his head were in flames. He whispered through his teeth.

"The warden's name was Hara, but he called himself Scorpion. I don't know what he looked like. He kept me blind-folded the whole time I was there because he didn't want me to see him. In the dream he has no face. And he has—he hasn't— he has no hands. He has a scorpion's pincers instead of hands. He holds his hammer in these pincer fingers. They ask me their question again and again and pound the nails into me, until my arm is full of nails. If I ever answer them, if I tell them what they want to know, they'll stop."

"What wakes you up?" Goewin asked quietly, her eyes still closed.

"I answer them," Telemakos whispered. "I tell them you

sent me. And then Anako dusts his hands and turns away, and tells the scorpion with no face to hammer a nail through my heart. Then I start screaming and wake myself up."

Goewin wiped her eyes angrily with the back of one hand, smoothing the shamma over her knees with the other.

"Anako will never come back to Aksum," she said. "He may already be dead of plague. Your own command sent him into exile."

She added fiercely, "Don't answer him, my sunbird."

"The infection's coming back," Telemakos whispered.

"How do you know?"

"I can smell it." He sighed, his sigh a whisper also, like dry leaves rustling. "I wish—"

He did not yet have the courage to speak his wish aloud, nor did he believe that anyone around him would have the courage to act on it.

The shamma in Goewin's lap began to squirm and whimper. Telemakos craned his neck and saw the shining bronze of his sister's hair, and one tiny fist the same fair brown as his own hands. The whimper rose to a wail.

"Hush, hush, you'll wake the house, you noisy little hoot owl," Goewin crooned. She stood up and hoisted the wailing bundle over her shoulder, jigging her gently up and down. She said softly, "Come walk with me in the garden, my owlet." She held the baby against her with one arm, and with the other she kissed the tips of her fingers and touched Telemakos's sound shoulder as her goodnight to him. Telemakos watched with longing and envy as Goewin carried his sister out of his bedroom.

Sunlight streamed through his window all the next day, dazzling him. Goewin came back in the afternoon and set a round glass bowl of colored water on his windowsill. She turned to look at him.

"Summer has come, Telemakos," she said sadly. "The fields are gold with Meskal daisies."

"What is that for?" he asked, nodding at the bowl.

"It's bait," Goewin said. "I got the idea from Gedar's wife Sesen, across the street. Wait and see what it catches."

Telemakos watched it glowing like a giant ruby on his windowsill over the next few days, as his fever rose and the nightmare nails through his arm bit at him so severely that he could not eat and could not sleep. Then it became too much of an effort to turn his head that way. He lay between sleep and waking, staring at the lions carved into the coffered ceiling, thinking about nothing. There was no room in his mind for any thought beyond the driving agony that had once been his left arm. He began to wish only that he would hurry up and die and get it over with.

The morning after it became too much effort for Telemakos to speak, Goewin did not go out to the New Palace. She sat by his side, not fussing with his dressings, not pacing, not weeping. The baby wailed sadly to herself in another room. They still had not bothered to give her a name.

Goewin got up quietly and went out to see to her.

III

ATHENA

WHEN GOEWIN CAME back she was jigging the little squirming, bronze-tipped bundle over her shoulders. She stopped suddenly in the doorway and hissed in a delighted whisper, "Oh, Telemakos, look at the window!"

There was a malachite sunbird perching on the edge of the bright bowl, its thin, curved bill just touching the surface of the honeyed water. Its wings shone iridescent emerald. It sipped there fearlessly, as if there were no one in the room.

"Goewin," Telemakos said, "I need you to do a thing for me."

They were the first words he had spoken in more than a day, and what he said then had been whispered. Now his voice suddenly sounded normal again, clear and determined.

"Are you better this morning?" Goewin asked in surprise.

"Nothing hurts anymore. I feel better," Telemakos said. "I'm not better. I'm dying."

Goewin stood silent for a moment, jogging the baby against her shoulder.

"I want my arm taken off," Telemakos said. "Make my father do it."

She answered fiercely, "Yes. All right."

"If Ras Meder won't do it himself, then get Amosi."

"All right. Give me an hour. I'll get your mother to sit with you." She turned to obey him, almost immediately.

"Wait!" Telemakos cried softly. "Goewin, wait. *Please* let me see the baby."

The sunbird raised its head and began to preen, balancing on the rim of the bowl with its long tail, a blaze of green above the crimson water.

"*Please*," Telemakos begged. "Put her down over here, on my right. I don't mind if she cries. I want to *see* her."

Goewin laid his sister gently at his side.

The baby looked up at him without whimpering. Her hair gleamed with the metallic sheen of bronze, while her skin was the even brown of roasted grain. Her hair smelled of sandalwood. It was not oiled with it; that was just the way it smelled, coincidence. She gazed at Telemakos steadily, her expression faintly worried. She had been crying, but her eyes were dry. She was so young she could not yet make tears when she wept. Her eyes were the clear gray of a winter sky.

"She has eyes just like Athena's," Telemakos said. "In *The Odyssey*."

"I've thought that too," Goewin said with a small, tired smile. "'The gray-eyed goddess,' Homer calls her."

"You honey," Telemakos whispered to the baby. She stared at him with her dry, bright eyes. "Oh, you honey. I wish I could hold you."

He could not even move to touch her. She seemed the smallest, most vivid creature he had ever seen, more vibrant even than Sheba and Solomon had been as cubs, because he could sense the latent intelligence looking out through her clear, gray eyes.

Telemakos looked up at Goewin. "Her name is Athena," he declared.

Goewin twisted her mouth into a weary smile and nodded. "You are right." She leaned down gently and lifted the baby onto her shoulder again. "I don't think either of your parents will contest that choice. And who knows, maybe it is a smoke screen I can use. The emperor calls his advisor Mentor, after all, not Athena, and if it is ever spoken abroad, it will seem to mean only the baby." Goewin blew out a sharp breath through pinched nostrils, like an angry sigh. "High time she had a name, as well, poor thing. I'm frustrated with your parents, Telemakos. Your mother lies in bed weeping half the day and no longer bothers to comb her hair; your father turns his back and walks out of the room if the baby is in it. If you die, I will leave this house and take your little Athena with me. But if you live—"

"I'll have to help you," Telemakos said. "I will, I promise."

Goewin went to find his father.

Ferem, the butler, came in quietly and began to set out the too-familiar physician's instruments on a clean white cloth; all except the small, narrow jeweler's saw, which he laid in the brazier. He knelt at Telemakos's side.

"God bless you, child."

He took Telemakos's hand, the sound one, and kissed it gently. "Your mother will be here in a moment," Ferem said, "and she'll stay till you're asleep. I will see you in the morning, when you wake up."

The second half of that week was not very different from the first. Telemakos was scarcely aware enough to realize what had happened to him; he lay half-dead as his body fought off the last of the infection. But the cruel nails were gone. Once he heard his aunt ask soberly, "How is it with our young lion tamer now?" There was quiet relief and firm confidence in his father's answer: "Much better."

Then one morning Telemakos woke up clear headed and ravenously hungry. He barely had the strength to shake the rattle that would bring Ferem; he had been kept alive over the last fortnight on little more than honey and water.

His mother came in. She had combed her hair or allowed someone to comb it for her: it was fixed out of her face in the familiar, neat rows of narrow plaits, billowing loose and full around the base of her neck. Telemakos felt as though he had not seen her for months, though her room was next to his.

"You've been lost! You've been lost!" he cried out to her. "I can't reach you. Kiss me again and again! Oh, come closer, I need you!"

"You don't," she said. "You need Medraut, and you need Goewin. All I do is feed people."

"I need you to hold me," Telemakos said plaintively.

But she was right: she had to feed him. Ferem propped him up so he could drink, and Turunesh held a bowl of broth to his lips.

"Ugh, this horrible British stock," Telemakos said. "Why do you let Goewin cook?"

It was delicious, though; it was as if he had never tasted food before.

"She's been fishing, south of the city, where the river Mai Barea grows so broad," his mother said. "She takes the baby with her."

"I'm not drinking fish paste soup if there's fresh trout in the kitchens," Telemakos said firmly. "I want it fried in pepper."

He did not get the pepper, but his mother gave in and let him have a tiny piece of fish, and mashed banana. She fed him patiently and wiped his mouth and dusted invisible crumbs off the bandages strapped across his chest. She was elaborate in keeping her attention strictly on his right side. Telemakos could tell that whatever was wrong with her had not gone away: she was not whole; she was not completely there.

He said, "This is the most wonderful food I've ever eaten. As soon as I can walk again, the first thing I will do is go down to the lake and catch my own dinner."

His mother collapsed across his legs with her face in her arms and burst into tears.

Telemakos was bewildered. He thought that fishing was something he could do, something that would make him feel normal again. Being able to walk through woodland five miles outside the city to his grandfather's fishing lodge seemed a reasonable goal to him, still yet a distant goal, but perhaps achievable before winter came again. And if he fixed his mind on that, it would make it easier to bear the terrible truth that he could not use a bow and could no longer hunt with his father.

But maybe I could learn to use a spear, Telemakos thought, while his mother wept hopelessly into his lap.

"Mother," Telemakos said softly, and managed to extract himself from beneath her weight so he could touch her hair. "Mother, don't cry. I'm so tired of not being able to move." He had spent the first two months of that year with his hands tied behind his back, and the last three in bed. It was too much for one year. He wanted to watch bushbuck grazing in the highland savannah, to play with Athena, to go back to drawing maps and learning the names of stars, to listen to the courtiers gossiping in the New Palace. He wanted to see the emperor's lions. They were modest pleasures and, Telemakos was sure, they were all within reach.

"I want a holiday," he said.

"What holiday shall you ever have?" his mother wept. "What will become of you, boy?"

"Mother, please don't cry. I hate it that I've made you so sad."

"It's not you," Turunesh said. "It's that wretched baby. You would not be lying here if not for her. I have no joy of her, ever. She never lets me sleep, she never stops weeping, she never smiles, she never thanks anyone—"

"She's a *baby*!" Telemakos interjected, shocked by this outburst and half inclined to laugh.

"I can't do anything for her. I can't do anything for you. Better she had never been born."

Ferem, who had been standing at the window, now said apologetically, "I must help your mother to her room, Telemakos. I'll come back."

Telemakos watched them go, his mother's bent shoulders shaking as the old man guided her out. He glanced down at his bare left side, at his shoulder and chest wrapped tightly in white bandages, and thought perhaps he should feel more unhappy. But he felt nothing but relief. His shoulder hurt, but it was clean, local pain. It did not spread up and down his body when he moved, and he did not have the dreadful, sick feeling that it would never go away until he let the faceless man with a scorpion's claws pound a nail through his heart.

I can go fishing, Telemakos thought contentedly, and I will.

* * *

The green sunbird continued to sip at the sweet water on the windowsill. Telemakos worked at being able to stand up. In another week he could walk from his bed to the window without having to stop and cling to the sill, gasping from exertion, before he started back. But it got easier.

He quickly grew bored with this circuit and began to make his way slowly through the house. His father was still so paranoid about the infection recurring that he posted guards at the outside doors to stop Telemakos from venturing into the garden; he could not be trusted to keep out of the fishpond or the stables.

One afternoon when Goewin was away, Athena cried to herself for so long that Telemakos thought there must be no one else alive in the entire city.

Oh, this awful *house,* he thought.

Eventually he could no longer stand to listen to it. He got up and put his head through to his mother's bedroom: she was asleep, or pretending to be asleep, with her head wrapped up in a shawl as though she were trying to suffocate herself. Telemakos assumed she was merely trying to stop her ears.

Why don't they get a nurse? Telemakos wondered. Grandfather makes all these empty threats about sending the baby away when he wants to scare my mother, but if no one wants to take care of Athena, why don't we just hire a nurse for her? We could afford a nurse, even if the plague quarantine has made Grandfather so parsimonious he won't buy new lamps when we break them. We could afford a dozen nurses. I had a nurse. I had a nurse for so long I was old enough to cut my name into a piece of cedar wood for her to remember me by when she left. I did it in Greek; it was when I started learning to read *The Odyssey*. I must have been at least seven years old.

It occurred to Telemakos that his parents had not paid much more attention to him as an infant than they did to his sister. His father had not even known of his existence for the first six years of Telemakos's life; his mother had continued her noblewoman's audiences and parties and the work she did for her father, with little change in her routine after Telemakos was born. It had been made clear to him on several occasions—though not by his mother, to be fair—that he was lucky not to have been sequestered on a clifftop or in a hermitage, as often happened to unwanted royal children.

But my mother wanted me, Telemakos thought. I reminded her of my father. That's why she kept me. And Athena only reminds them of my accident.

He followed the sound of the baby's frustrated, abandoned screams. The nursery was next to his mother's room, and Athena lay shrieking and sobbing in a large palm basket raised to the level of the window. Evidence of Goewin's presence was all about the room. She had hung copper chimes in this window, also; they clinked and tinkled in the summer wind from the Simien Mountains. Big, brightly colored beads were strung across the cradle.

Telemakos leaned over so that his face was close to the baby's and said softly, "Hello, little sister."

Instantly she stopped crying. He put out a finger, and she held tightly to it, all of her tiny fingers wound firmly around one of his. She was able to cry tears now, and her deep gray eyes were wet, but so bright they seemed to sparkle. Telemakos stared into them and found himself incurably in love.

"Come here, hoot owl," he whispered. "Oh, you stink. Small wonder you're howling."

He scooped her up without thinking about it. He slipped his sound right arm beneath her from the bottom up, cupping her head in his hand, and swooped her over his left shoulder so that his arm was crossed over his chest. She let out a whooping hiccup of a gasp as she landed. She was tight and secure against him that way, but he was not prepared for the pressure her head put on his newly healed wounds.

"*Aiee.*"

He gasped and sat down hard on the floor, but held her tight.

"Oh, you're *hurting* me, you little slug—" He bit his lip. It was his own fault. "All right. We'll move you. Come on—" He wanted to move her carefully, but he was *so clumsy.* He had to gather all his strength and then sling her from one side of him to the other. Again she let out a shrieking hiccup. She was less secure held this way, but he did not have the strength to hold her otherwise.

Her small body was still now, as if to be held against

him—or anyone—was the only thing she ever wanted. After a minute or so he collected himself and struggled to his feet. He could not lever or pull himself up as long as he was clinging to the baby. He fought against his own slight body, pulled down by Athena's added weight, and found his sense of balance all skewed as well. He made it to one knee, fell back, climbed up again, and finally staggered upright. Athena gasped and choked with her crazy little hiccups.

She was laughing.

Every giddy dive and swoop made her yelp with rudimentary laughter. Telemakos leaned back against the wall and closed his eyes, triumphant and exhausted, clutching the baby against his chest. By the time he had stopped gasping for breath, his arm was aching with strain.

"I'm going to have to put you down," he told his sister. He glanced quickly around the room. Everything in the nursery was alien to him. "I'm going to have to put you back in your bed. You're still a stinker, but I'll clean you up, all right? It will probably take me the rest of the afternoon."

He did not know where any of her things were or what you did with them or how they worked. Athena began to whimper the second Telemakos let go of her; she was hysterical with fury long before he had even managed to get her dirty napkin off. She pulled her little legs up into her stomach and balled her brown, dimpled hands into tiny fists, screaming in great, long, choking waves. Telemakos fought her doggedly, absolutely as stubborn as she was.

"Do you *be quiet!*" he yelled at her at last. "I cannot help you any faster than this. *I have only got one arm!*"

"Telemakos."

He fastened the last fold he had made, tightening the knotted cloth with his teeth. It was crude, and probably uncomfortable, but the baby was clean. Telemakos straightened and glanced over his shoulder. Goewin stood in the doorway.

"Let me help," she offered quietly.

"Too late!"

He was slick with sweat, though he had long since pulled off his shamma and now wore only a kilt. He said proudly, "I'm finished."

He sat down on the floor again, thoroughly spent. Goewin lifted the sobbing baby up over her own shoulder and asked, "Where in blazes is your mother?"

"Asleep."

"Don't be ridiculous. The two of you would wake the dead."

"She takes my opium."

Goewin gazed down at Telemakos, who sat panting at her feet, sweating beneath his bandages. He looked away from the calculating assessment in his aunt's dark eyes. He was too dark skinned to blanch with pain or effort, but he knew he must be gray around the mouth and that Goewin would not miss the tightness in his jaw or the slight trembling that ran all through his body.

"God blind me, Telemakos, you are the image of your father

sometimes," Goewin muttered under her breath. "Look, boy, I haven't the strength to carry you and the baby at once. Can you get back to bed yourself?"

"In a minute."

"I'll tell Ferem to come and bathe you."

She stood gazing down at him while he caught his breath. Athena still let out a racking sob every few seconds, but it was not real crying: she, too, was catching her breath. Goewin watched Telemakos with sharp eyes as he dragged himself slowly to his feet again.

"About that opium," she said.

"She takes it because I never use it."

"Idiot."

"Me or her?"

"Both of you." Goewin herded Telemakos down the hall before her. He sat down on his own bed and thought, I will be asleep before Ferem gets here.

"Don't try to clean the baby again," Goewin said to him. "Anyone of the household will do that, if you ask. They can't hear her from the kitchens or the stables. It's not a bad thing for you to help with her, but it will be a pyrrhic victory if you poison yourself in doing it. You will die, Telemakos, *you will die*, if you infect yourself again. There isn't any more of you to cut away."

She turned her back and went to find the butler.

A day later Telemakos was in Athena's room again, swooping her up over his shoulder once more. He took her back to bed with him, propped her against his hip, and shored her there with cushions so that she could see the sunbird at the window. Athena's small, uncoordinated hands moved slowly, grasping for the far, bright feathers and the bright water; then her hands distracted her and she stared at them as if there could be nothing more fascinating. She tried to put them in her mouth and missed.

Telemakos gave her the sistrum that he used to summon Ferem. It looked like something that had been stolen from a church, possibly liberated from the monastery at Abba Pantelewon by his father. It was a fork of mahogany with shining silver bells threaded on wires between the tines. Athena reached for it, missed, and reached again. She moved her hands with slow deliberation, purposefully, but without skill. The fingers of her right hand closed around the sistrum's handle as if by accident. The polished wood was the same color as her hand. It was too heavy for her to hold if Telemakos let go, but she shook it so that the bells chattered faintly. It surprised her, and she let out her funny little hiccup of delight.

"Clever girl!" Telemakos laughed also, and gently pulled the rattle away. "Do it again."

This time she caught it in her left hand.

"Both hands!" Telemakos crowed. "Well done. Clever girl—" He faltered suddenly. "Lucky girl," he whispered. "Well done, lucky girl."

When the baby began to whimper with hunger, Telemakos hid her under his blankets, letting her suck on his fingers to keep her quiet while Ferem brought him a bowl of milk. When they were alone again, Telemakos fed his sister with a napkin twisted into a makeshift teat. It took at least an hour. In the evening Medraut found his children curled against each other, sound asleep.

After that they gave up trying to keep the baby away from Telemakos.

IV

THE LURE OF SHADOWS

"THERE," MEDRAUT SAID, running the tips of his fingers along the blind seam in Telemakos's shoulder. "Finished. And your skin should grow with you comfortably; you can thank Amosi for that. Your grandmother the queen of the Orcades could not have made cleaner work of it, and that's saying something. Let me show you."

The bandages were gone. Medraut held one of Turunesh's mirrors at Telemakos's back, and Telemakos held another, so he could see behind him.

"We did not ever cut through bone in the end," Medraut explained. "We took your arm straight out of its socket, at the join with your shoulder."

Telemakos tilted the mirror back and forth, fascinated. His ribs and throat were impressively scarred as well, back and front.

"Solomon never took his teeth out of your arm," Medraut

explained. "The other wounds on your body were made by his claws. They were ugly, and any one of them could have killed you if it had festered, but they were not deep." Medraut's low, musical voice was matter-of-fact as he laid out these horrors. "You did the right thing, Telemakos."

"I did?"

"You kept the lion's teeth away from your throat. You sacrificed your arm for it, but that is what saved your life. Well, that, and Nezana forcing Sheba off so she could not open you up while her partner held you down."

Telemakos choked back a sob, feeling sorry for himself: not because he had lost his arm, but because he knew he would never be allowed in the lion pit again.

"Does it hurt?" Medraut asked.

"Nothing hurts." Telemakos sniffed. "I miss my lions."

"They aren't your lions, boy." Medraut's tone was dry.

He added, gentler now, "It's said lost limbs cause pain that isn't really there. You seem to do a lot of desperate flailing when you move; you've lost your grace."

"I have trouble balancing," Telemakos admitted. "I try to move my arm, and there isn't anything to move. I keep thinking I must be bound, as I was in Afar, and when I try to lift my arm, I can't. So I struggle."

Medraut laid aside the mirror. He looked down at his own scarred hands, and at the blue physician's mark of Asclepius tattooed in his left palm. He murmured, "I don't know how to heal you of the wounds you took in Afar."

Telemakos said, surprised, "They're long healed. They were nothing."

"I don't mean these," Medraut said, tapping lightly at Telemakos's scarred fingertips, where Hara had slashed the nails off to assure Anako that Telemakos was mute. "I mean the wounds to your spirit, which make you scream in the dark, and trick your body into believing it is still being forcibly subdued. Do you dream about the lions?"

"Never."

"Well, Solomon crippled you. Hara the Scorpion did not. Who torments you in your sleep?"

Without warning Medraut laid his hand across Telemakos's eyes.

Telemakos gasped and shuddered, flinching.

"You see," Medraut said.

Telemakos was appalled. He had not thought his secret fears were so transparent.

Medraut spoke more to himself than to Telemakos, his musical voice dark with menace. "I swear, when we round up the last of these salt pirates, I will demand their heads struck up on pikes in the Cathedral Square. That will bring an end to the tale. That will see you avenged."

"I don't need avenging," Telemakos said. "Or I'd be angry at Solomon, too."

"Oh, aye, that's what you'd do, turn the other cheek. If your friend the lion should eat up your left arm, offer to him the other also."

Telemakos laughed. Medraut gave a faint smile with half his mouth. Encouraged to hear his father quoting scriptures of forgiveness, albeit loosely and with sarcasm, Telemakos stood up and twisted his shamma over his shoulders. "Sir, you yourself bear a grudge against a person who does not deserve your ill will any more than Solomon deserves mine," he said boldly. "Wait here for me a minute."

He left his father in his bedroom while he went into the nursery.

Athena was just awake. She woke quietly of late, because now that her hands worked for her she was able to grasp at the beads and toys hanging over her face, and they kept her entertained until someone more interesting came along. Telemakos loved the look of her eyes when they met his after she had been asleep. They glinted like sunlight on water, as if everything in the world held unlimited excitement and expectation.

He could lift her easily now. She was heavier, but not much, and he was considerably stronger. He hoisted her over his shoulder and took her back to their father.

Medraut stood up, but Telemakos barred his way. Medraut glared at him through narrowed storm-blue eyes.

"Stop blaming her for my accident," Telemakos said. "It was my own fault."

"I cannot love her," Medraut answered. His deep, melodious voice was cold and flat.

"Only look at her," Telemakos insisted, and edged aside so Medraut could see the baby's face.

She was nearly seven months old now. She was not a big baby, but she held her head up with such alert and intense interest, and had such a thick shock of springing, burning hair, that she seemed much older than she was.

Medraut held out the stiff, arthritic little finger of his left hand. Athena grasped it firmly with her own unthinkably small fingers, blindly trusting and certain.

"*All who are born have a right to be,*" Medraut murmured to himself, but then he shook away the baby's hand sharply and repeated, in a low voice, "God help me, but I cannot love her."

"Just . . . Do you have to love her? Just live with her, call her by her name. Here's what you can do," Telemakos said. "Tell Amosi to stop sending me opium. I don't use it, and it's pure evil to use that stuff on Athena."

For half a second, Telemakos thought his father was going to strike him.

But Medraut spoke with icy control. "Not I, boy. No one has ever been that desperate to keep her quiet."

"Not on purpose," Telemakos said. "But Mother still suckles her, sometimes."

"For God's sake." Medraut relaxed, and sighed. "So she does. All right—it's time we put a stop to that addiction, anyway. This wretched *house.*"

Everybody cursed Grandfather's house when there were no other convenient scapegoats left. Telemakos liked the house and felt sorry for it. Like Athena, it had not done anything.

◆　◆　◆

He went fishing with his grandfather. Telemakos and Kidane had quite a formal relationship, partly because Kidane sat on the emperor's private council and was usually even busier than Goewin, and partly because Kidane had always been the ultimate authority over Telemakos's behavior. When Telemakos was younger, his grandfather had never hesitated to have him whipped for his more serious transgressions. It was Kidane who had seen to it that Telemakos knew how to deport himself appropriately in a roomful of courtiers. But Telemakos liked his grandfather, who was noble and broadminded, and who had taught him how to listen. So they went fishing together, taking bedrolls and a small sack of tef flour so that they could camp for a few days even if they failed to catch anything.

It made Telemakos feel reborn to be outside the city. The highland fields were yellow with ripe grain, and the snow-capped Simien Mountains beckoned from the far horizon. The sounds and smells of the woodland river valley were intoxicating: chattering monkeys, screaming hornbills, the hooting hyena's yelp. Grandfather relaxed out of his role of councilor and disciplinarian and spent long, wet hours instructing Telemakos in the art of poling the reed-built canoe.

"Don't try to lift the pole the whole way out," Kidane suggested. "You can do that with two hands, but it's too long to do it with one. Try tipping it end over end, like the spoke of a wheel."

Telemakos was slow, and he was not strong enough to keep it up for long, but he could do it.

"Will you teach me how to throw a spear?" Telemakos asked Kidane.

"I don't know how to throw a spear," his grandfather answered. "I'm no huntsman. Ask your father."

They ate trout Telemakos gutted himself, using a flat rock as a butcher block, holding each fish down with his left knee and his right toes as he carefully cut loose the shining head and slit the silver belly to pull out its backbone. It was not the neatest work he had ever done, but it was without a doubt the most satisfying. He and Kidane slept contentedly through three black, still nights in the frail fishing lodge with walls of woven reed.

They were woken in the blue light before dawn on the fourth morning of their holiday by a lion roaring, the sound carrying with all the huge reverberation of rolling thunder. It was at least a mile away, but it sounded as though it were just the other side of the thin wall.

"Child, you're quaking," Grandfather said softly. They had both started bolt upright. Somewhere, not far off, a family of frightened baboons shrieked and scolded. Kidane pulled Telemakos's blanket up around his shoulders.

Telemakos sat rigid, eyes wide and nostrils flared.

"He's not so near as he sounds," Kidane said soothingly.

"I know. I'm not afraid of lions," Telemakos whispered. "But the smell . . ."

He shivered again, and knew that his father was right about the wounds to his spirit.

"What smell?" Kidane said.

"Can you not smell the baboons?" Telemakos whispered. "Anako smelled like that. There is nothing to be afraid of. But still it makes me want to be sick."

"You're hungry," Grandfather said practically. "Let's make breakfast."

Grandfather pulled on his shamma, climbed down the short catwalk that led outside from the sleeping platform, and began to rake at the ashes of last night's fire. "Bring the pan and flour," he called to Telemakos.

Telemakos wound his own shamma over his shoulders, feeling caught in tendrils of nightmare. He could still smell baboon. His ruined shoulder twitched as he clenched and unclenched the muscles in his back, trying to free the arm that was not there from bonds that were not there. Telemakos clamped his teeth together to keep them still and lifted the lid from the flour basket.

The half-empty sack inside lay folded neatly upon itself. Telemakos nearly reached in to pick it up, but the shadow in the fold was moving, a tiny clot of darkness shifting and reforming like a spot before his eyes. He pulled back with a low cry of surprise and loathing. It was a scorpion.

"Telemakos?"

He heard his grandfather call his name in concern, but it did not occur to him to answer. Telemakos watched the little, dangerous creature blundering about among the dark folds of cloth. He wondered, What does it feel like, a scorpion's sting?

It's so small. It can't hurt as much as a lion's teeth, can it, something so lightweight?

Hara's scorpion's pincers had held him lightly too, before wedging the knife's point beneath his fingernails.

Telemakos came at it from behind, prodding the back of its curved tail with one of his scarred fingertips. The barbed whip lashed out at nothing, and Telemakos backed away.

Grandfather was at his side again, slapping his fingers sharply.

"You surely know better than that, boy!"

Telemakos bent, staring at the flour sack, watching the shadows.

"Mother of God," Grandfather swore under his breath. He slammed the lid down on the basket, then took Telemakos by the back of his neck and drove him out of the hut. He marched his grandson straight down the bank and over his knees into Mai Barea, and threw a potful of river water into Telemakos's face.

"Ai, Grandfather, stop!"

Kidane lowered the pot.

"Are you awake yet?" he asked gruffly. "Come and help me make breakfast, then. I'll take care of the flour." He did not mention the awful thing inhabiting the flour sack, but he asked, "Were you stung?"

"I'm all right," Telemakos said.

Grandfather let out a sigh of relief. "We'll go home today, I think," he said quietly.

• • •

Goewin laughed as Kidane and Telemakos began to unpack their baskets of trout in the courtyard.

"What were you trying to do, feed the five thousand?"

"I said I could fish."

"So you did. Come with me to take some to Gedar."

In the two and a half years since the plague quarantine had been in place, forbidding all foreign trade, half the merchants' mansions in Grandfather's neighborhood had fallen derelict. In the villa across the street, Gedar's family still lived in two salvaged rooms without any cooks or gardeners or animals bigger than chickens. Goewin took it upon herself to bring them a barrel of flour every month, and coffee, and a parcel of honeycomb from the monastery at Abba Pantelewon.

"I've just got home," Telemakos said. "I want to see Athena."

"Bring her with you," answered Goewin. "She likes going out."

"I can't carry her that far."

"What rubbish. You carried fifteen pounds of trout the whole way back from the lake, didn't you? Athena isn't any heavier. Let me show you how to wrap the carrying cloth. It's much easier to carry her on your hip than over your shoulder."

V

LOAVES AND FISHES

IT WAS A SMALL battle to get the squirming, anxious baby to cooperate. Athena was interested in the fish. She kept trying to dive and grab at the basket while Goewin tried to tie her up. Goewin could not quite work out how to make the carrying cloth fit Telemakos, and he, awkwardly, could not hold Athena in place against his hip or tie the knots himself. But at last they got the baby fixed tightly against his left side, leaving free his right. Athena wound both hands into his hair.

"Help me, Goewin. Ai! Pull your own hair, you monster!" The baby's hands were too close to his head for him to be able to see them. "I shall teach you to comb it for me, if you like it so much."

Goewin, watching, suddenly laughed in delight.

"Now you know what it's like," she said. "That is just how I've spent the past seven months, little better off than you. Baby under one arm, trying to draw maps and make your soup and fold clean napkins with the other. You owe me, boy." She tickled Athena beneath her chin and kissed her behind one ear. "You both owe me, owlet."

They crossed the street together, Goewin carrying the fish and Telemakos carrying the baby. Goewin put down her basket to strike the bell at Gedar's gate; the neighbor children opened to them. Their shabby clothes were clean, and bitter pride smoldered in the eyes of the two elder boys as they went down on their knees before Goewin. The youngest did not bow.

"Get up, Sabarat," said Goewin. "And you, Japheth. I've told you before, you need not kneel to me. Is your mother in?"

"Mother and Father are both in," said Sabarat, the eldest, with blank politeness. As far as Telemakos knew, Mrs. Gedar never went out, but Gedar was always trying to drum up business in the city's markets; Sabarat, who was nearly a grown man now, usually went with him.

"How fortunate, we may all visit, then," said Goewin. "You can carry this basket."

"I beg you wait only a moment, Woyzaro Goewin, my lady ambassador," apologized Sabarat. "Mother will want to serve you coffee, but I beg you let me announce you before you go in. Father is going to Himyar, and we are in an uproar of packing."

"To Himyar!" Goewin said. "Are they still authorizing ships to leave the port in Adulis, then?"

Sabarat looked surprised. "More now than ever before. Don't you hear such things from Counselor Kidane? Your quarantine is to be lifted at winter's end. Father is going to travel to Himyar before the Long Rains begin, so that he may collect payment he has been due many years now, and be among the first let back in Aksum in the new year."

"That will be hard on your mother, to be without him for a whole season."

Sabarat gazed politely at his feet. "Oil of his olive groves used to light the alabaster palaces of Himyar," Sabarat said, the bitterness flaring beneath the politeness, "as well as the New Palace here in the city. But now we don't even know if those groves still exist."

"I don't know if my father's kingdom still exists," Goewin answered.

"My lady." Sabarat heaved the basket of fish over his shoulder. "Forgive me."

"If your father is planning to be first back in Aksum, perhaps I can persuade him to collect my mail on his way through Adulis. I long for news of my homeland. We are all weary of the quarantine."

Sabarat took the basket up the podium stairs, which were swept clean as always. Mrs. Gedar was house proud. But the courtyard was littered with last year's almond leaves, and the fountains were dry.

Japheth and little Eon both stood facing Telemakos now, watching with curiosity as Athena tried to hide in his shamma. She was shy; her everyday existence only included about five different faces. "Is that your sister?" Japheth asked. "Her hair is not so strange as yours, is it?"

"It is not," Telemakos agreed. He had endured insults directed at his white hair and slate-blue eyes as long as he could remember.

"You are like a scorpion, carrying its young on its back," said Japheth. Eon, used to the game of name-calling, sang out boldly: "Scorpion, scorpion, scorpion boy—run away, Japheth, the scorpion's going to sting us!"

Athena lifted her head to watch this noisy performing creature. After a moment she pointed to the house, where the fish had disappeared, and babbled with incomprehensible concern about them.

"Little scorpion baby," sang Eon to Athena. He made his hands into pincers, his fingers separated two and two together, and gently jabbed these claws into the firm, swaddled bump that was Athena's body.

Telemakos's heart went cold. Abruptly he lifted his single hand to fend off the attack. Eon's nails raked his open palm.

Telemakos seized the little boy's hand and jerked it back upon itself, and only Goewin's cool fingers twined forcefully about his wrist kept him from trying to break Eon's arm.

"Telemakos," Goewin said softly at his ear. She shook Eon Gedar from Telemakos's trembling grip. "Do not hurt this child."

Japheth had caught his brother by the shoulders and now held him back, furiously scolding him while gasping apologies that were directed as much at Goewin as at Telemakos. Goewin spoke calmly in Telemakos's ear, using his formal title like a whip.

"The correct apology is for you to make, *Lij Telemakos*."

It meant "young prince." Only the emperor used it with any frequency. It always sobered Telemakos to hear it spoken aloud.

He stood panting, his heart slowing again to its normal pace. His knees felt as though they had turned to water. He bent his head to Athena, holding her close, and brushed his flaming face against her coppery hair. After a moment Telemakos knelt before Gedar's children with his head bowed.

"Stop making Eon scream, Japheth, the fault is mine."

"Telemakos is bodyguard to his sister, you see," Goewin commented coolly.

Then Sabarat came back to usher them in to coffee. Goewin helped Telemakos up with one hand supporting Athena, then offered her arm to him so that he might formally escort her into the house. She kept her cool fingers twined through his until he stopped shaking.

Gedar's reception hall was like Grandfather's seen through a dark mirror. It was orderly and clean, if crowded with the debris of daily living, but ruin preyed on the house. The plaster wash was peeling from the walls, the oil lamps were empty, the stone floors cold and bare. It smelled of dust and faint decay.

Gedar exclaimed and smiled over the gift of food. He managed to make himself ingratiating without ever actually saying thank you.

"Beautiful fish! Where did you get such a quantity? How we shall enjoy them. I must go myself one day, though of course I have no right to my own stretch of riverbank, unlike the emperor's counselors."

Sesen, his wife, was fussing over the coffee burner, but she looked up to exclaim warmly, "Telemakos Meder! How nice to see you on your feet! And the baby is getting so big!"

The baby had found his hair again. Telemakos held himself stiffly formal as Sesen began the brewing ritual.

She offered coffee to Telemakos, but he was not allowed it by his mother, and because Goewin was watching, he had to refuse it. He and Gedar's sons stood politely facing the walls while the adults drank and Athena tried to drag Telemakos's hair out of his scalp. Then she began chewing on his hair, which was too disgusting to bear. He jerked his head aside and tried to distract her.

"Look, Mrs. Gedar has got a sunbird trap like ours," Telemakos whispered. It was the only ornament in the room, a chipped dish containing the same red-dyed honey-water that Goewin had put in Telemakos's window. He edged closer so Athena could see. The water had not been changed for a long time and was leaving a rim of sticky dye and trapped insects around the edge of the dish as it evaporated.

Athena swooped at the beguiling mess. Telemakos backed away quickly and tried a different game.

"Nose," he whispered, touching her nose. "Point to your nose."

She stabbed him in the face with a small, accurate brown finger.

"That's my nose, Athena, not yours," he whispered patiently. "Here's yours. . . ." He made her touch her nose. "Now where's your chin?"

She thumped his chin.

"Telemakos Meder, you are a martyr," Goewin commented. "Take her out to the courtyard. She likes the chickens."

"Ceremony is tiresome for children, isn't it?" Gedar said. "Especially little ones. Come with me, Telemakos." He rose to his feet and gestured the way before him with an open hand. Telemakos picked his way cautiously across the crowded room, a little unbalanced by the restless baby on his hip. Gedar's sons turned their eyes toward him to watch him go, but they had not been invited to come along.

"Let's find a toy for your sister, Telemakos Meder."

Gedar did not lead Telemakos outside. He wove his way through the dim mansion, along disused corridors and galleries, until they came to a narrow, dark room like a vault in the middle of the house, lit only by an air shaft.

"This is my treasury," Gedar said. "Most of it mere trinkets now."

There was a faded green basket on Gedar's accounting table. He lifted its woven lid and dipped a hand inside. "What have I got here for little girls? Ah, look at this!"

Unexpectedly, he fished out a baby's bracelet hung with silver charms.

There were five of them, tiny waterbirds: crane, ibis, pelican, flamingo, gull. Gedar held the pretty jingling thing up to

Athena. She did not immediately try to eat it; she watched it swing, and tapped it to make the charms shiver.

"It was my wife's, when she was a child," Gedar told Telemakos.

"We can't take such a gift," Telemakos protested.

"We have no girls," said Gedar. "And we are indebted to the house of Nebir. A present to a baby is a small thing. I know it pleases your aunt to be charitable, but we must make some return."

Gedar let Athena take the bracelet. She put it in her mouth. Telemakos pulled it away from her face, embarrassed.

"She is a little plague of locusts all on her own," he apologized. "She eats everything. Look at these little *birds*, my owlet! Remember the sunbird that comes to my window?"

Gedar chuckled. Then he lifted a cover of palm matting that lay beneath his accounting table and laid bare a small stack of amole, the valued blocks of cut salt that were the standard alternative to gold. He laid a loaf of salt on the table and set about carving a bar of manageable size off one end.

"For you, lad," Gedar said.

Telemakos objected fiercely. "Oh, I must not. The little bracelet is too much anyway. Goewin would never allow me—"

"It is nothing to do with her. You caught the fish. This is my payment for it."

Athena tried to feed her bracelet to Telemakos, and he held her off, watching Gedar saw through the amole. In Gebre Meskal's service Telemakos had become a judge of salt, and he saw that this of Gedar's was very fine, and that the loaf was stamped with Abreha Anbessa's seal, a lion's head encircled by a five-pointed star.

How has Gedar come by the royal salt of Himyar? Telemakos wondered. He must have been hoarding it for years, since the days when his olive oil lit Abreha's palace. He has sold his horses and his household goods, and dismissed all his servants, and is giving away his wife's jewelry, but he's saved his salt.

"Shouldn't you keep this yourself," Telemakos murmured, "in case you should need it?"

"Children shouldn't worry over such things," Gedar answered. "All will be repaired, soon enough."

Or it could be counterfeit, Telemakos thought. He knew that the corrupt warden of the mines at Afar had had other schemes besides avoiding the quarantine. Telemakos had heard the workers muttering about Hara's sidelines.

Hara, the warden at Afar. Telemakos found his eyes burning. *God, how I hated him*, he thought. *Scorpion*. He used to spit in the water they gave me, knowing I would drink it or die of thirst.

"Let this be a secret between us," Gedar said, tying the small salt tablet into a corner of Telemakos's shamma. "Your aunt need never know. There will be salt aplenty in the new year, when Gebre Meskal throws wide his gates. Abreha the Lion Hunter remembers his debts. And so do I." He took the bracelet from Athena and fastened it around her wrist. She shook her fist furiously up and down, making the silver charms ring.

"Thank you, sir," Telemakos said, trying to smile blandly, knowing he could not honorably refuse the gift. "You are very kind."

He looked up, then, and held Athena's wrist still for a moment, to stop the jangling. "Your son is looking for you," Telemakos said.

Gedar stepped into the passage. Telemakos cast a final glance at the salt loaf on the table, with the king of Himyar's mark on it. He did not think it was counterfeit; the salt was too good.

Telemakos followed Gedar into the corridor.

"Here, by the treasury, Japheth," Gedar called.

"Father? *Father?*"

Japheth appeared around one of the dim corners. He was feeling his way, and he was very loud. Telemakos saw that he was frightened of the dark, and the dust, afraid of his own house. Telemakos felt sorry for him.

"Stop shouting, Japheth," Gedar said mildly. "What is it?"

"Ras Meder and the lady Woyzaro Turunesh are here now, too. . . ."

"Oh." Gedar heaved a small sigh, and turned it into a chuckle. "A party."

Telemakos looked away, embarrassed.

"Sir—" Japheth glanced at Telemakos, then lowered his eyes respectfully before his father. "Woyzaro Turunesh is . . . upset. She's looking for her children, and Ras Meder her husband wants her to return home." Japheth's eyes met Telemakos's this time, and for one astonishing moment, the two of them were united in sympathy at each other's ghastly parents. "You'd better come to her," Japheth said to Telemakos directly. "She's out front."

"Thank you," Telemakos said.

Medraut had caught Turunesh in Gedar's courtyard. He must have chased her all the way through Grandfather's fore-court, across the street, and through Gedar's gate before he got hold of her. Now he stood behind her with his arms locked around her shoulders, imprisoning her by the wrists with her own arms crossed over her chest. Goewin stood before them with Turunesh's face clasped tenderly between her hands. She whispered something at her friend's ear through the wild hair. All Gedar's family stood by gawking; even the chickens seemed to be staring.

Telemakos braced the back of Athena's head protective-ly against his chest and ran to his mother. Goewin stepped away and Medraut let go of one of Turunesh's wrists, so that Telemakos could take her hand.

"Mother, I'm here. Look, I have the baby with me, too. See what Gedar's given her?" He stretched Athena's arm out, and she shook her silver bracelet. "Isn't it lovely? She's never had a decoration before—" As Turunesh grew calmer Medraut let go of her other hand, and she gripped Telemakos's shamma.

"Where did the scorpion touch you?"

"*Turunesh Kidane!*" Goewin hissed.

Telemakos stood appalled, held fast by his mother's clutching hands.

Medraut said sharply, "She overheard your grandfather telling me of your adventure this morning, Telemakos."

Goewin drew a quick breath and did not let it go, her mouth half-opened. Telemakos shook his head silently, not understanding. Athena had spotted the chickens now and was bobbing her head and clucking in imitation of them; Telemakos watched her without seeing her.

"Of the visitor you had in your flour sack, boy," Medraut reminded his son, but glared at Goewin as he spoke. She was not easily caught off guard. "Your mother heard Kidane speaking of the scorpion you found, and thought you might have been stung. Not satisfied with your grandfather's pledges of your sound health, we've all come running over here to see for ourselves."

"Oh," Telemakos gasped in great relief, and laughed, comprehension coming back. Athena was *so funny*. She shook her head vigorously up and down along with the hens as they pecked at bugs in the dust. It was like being pulled to pieces, trying to cope with her and his mother at the same time. "I wasn't hurt at all, I'm fine, Mother! How you worry!"

Then Gedar's wife made a valiant effort to preserve her neighbor's dignity. "Ah, Turunesh Kidane," Sesen said, and came forward to kiss Turunesh on the cheek. "I can see why you should worry, when Telemakos Meder has been ill so long, and this his first time out in the wide world again. What a joy it must be that he is well. And able to help with the baby, too, clever lad. It's a blessing he was not crippled, or worse."

Turunesh looked down at Athena, and then at her husband. She and Medraut stared at each other, seeing and understanding something no one else saw or understood.

Sesen finished warmly, "Take care of your lovely sister, Telemakos."

"You see it?" Turunesh said, and she was speaking only to Medraut. "Do you realize? The baby hides his arm. He looks like anyone else carrying a baby. So long as she's there with him, no one will ever notice!"

Medraut gazed at Athena as if he were seeing her for the first time. Turunesh was right. None of Gedar's family had noticed anything wrong with Telemakos, not even Japheth and Eon. All afternoon there had been not one remark about his missing arm. There had been no staring, no whispering.

Telemakos understood, too.

"Indeed, Sesen, my mother's friend, I will take care of my lovely sister," he vowed.

Medraut said, "We all will."

VI

HOPE

TELEMAKOS STRUGGLED IN his sleep with such violence, trying to escape his tormenters, that he ended up halfway across his bedroom. He had managed to tangle himself so securely in the bedclothes that he could not free his face. He lay on the floor screaming, *"Take it off! Take it off!"* until his father came in and tore the blanket nearly in half.

Medraut held Telemakos against him without speaking while Ferem made up the bed again. Medraut's rough cheek was cool against Telemakos's temple. Athena wailed in her room across the hall.

"I wonder what she dreams about," Telemakos whispered.

"Hunting for milk, probably," Medraut murmured close to his ear.

They sat quietly on the floor together. Turunesh came in with the baby snuffling against her shoulder. She sat down with them and let Athena suckle.

Telemakos lay curled with his head in his father's lap and his back pressed against his mother's side, and had nearly drifted to sleep again when Medraut started to lift him up to help him back to bed. Telemakos started awake suddenly, whimpering.

"Take the baby to sleep with you," Turunesh said. "It makes you both calmer."

She settled them together. Athena bunched herself up like a small animal, with her arms and knees pulled up beneath her, her face turned aside so she could snuggle against Telemakos. He had never heard any sound so peaceful as her gusty, quiet snore. Turunesh kissed them each on the forehead before she left.

Medraut made a saddle for Athena to ride in so that Telemakos could carry her at his side without having to tie her in the carrying cloth. The new harness had a supporting strap held in place by a sleeve over Telemakos's right shoulder, and a belt around his hips so that the baby's weight did not strain his back. Athena would be able to climb in and out of the saddle herself when Telemakos unfastened the buckles.

It took Medraut several days of concentration to make the saddle. He sat on the edge of the fish pool in the garden court behind the house, stitching pieces of leather together and keeping Athena nearby so he could measure her every so often. The fish fascinated her. She stood by the rim of the pool, watching them dart back and forth, or smacking the surface of the water to make them start away. Medraut tethered her by the waist to a date palm so that she could reach the pond but not him. He cracked strips of antelope hide like a whip against the granite paving blocks if she came too close. He had caught her fingers once, and she kept clear of his work now.

This afternoon she crawled round and round the trunk of the palm until she was stuck there, and sat digging in the dirt at the foot of the tree for a few minutes before she carefully untangled herself. Telemakos watched her, fascinated, from the podium stairway at the back of the house, where she could not see him. She wound and unwound herself around the tree three times.

When Telemakos finally came toward her, she crawled to the fishpond and pulled herself up to the rim. There she stood screaming frantically, "TatatataTATATA!"

The first time she had greeted him this way, Telemakos had thought, with a surge of delight, that she was trying to say his name. But he soon realized that, in fact, she was trying to say her own name.

He sat on the pool's rim between his father and his sister.

"Will you teach me to throw a spear?" Telemakos asked his father.

Medraut looked up. "I have not the ability. I am trained as an archer and a swordsman."

"You were Gebre Meskal's ceremonial spear bearer in the royal hunt, when he first became emperor. And you killed the lion whose skin hangs in the reception hall."

"That, too, was a royal hunt. It was a test. I had to prove myself a worthy representative of my father the high king in the Aksumite court. Abreha did the same when he became king of Himyar, which is why his nobles call him 'Lion Hunter' now. No Himyarite before him had to pass such a test; it is a custom of the Aksumite kings.

"You have no such challenge to rise to," Medraut finished. "If the emperor wants you for his warrior, he will give you a spear, and show you how to use it."

"I, a warrior?" Telemakos said, and laughed. "I want to hunt with you. It doesn't have to be lions."

"It is no jest," Medraut said seriously. He looked down again, and picked up his work. "I have this for you," he said, and Telemakos saw that it was a sling, woven of intricately plaited strands of dark wool. "It will afford you some protection, and small prey if you are accurate."

Medraut lifted a cloth that lay among his tailor's equipment, uncovering a bowl of dried dates. He picked this up and set it between himself and Telemakos on the edge of the pool. Athena inched along the stone rim until she was leaning against Telemakos's knees, gazing at the dates. Telemakos did not think she realized they were food; they were simply shiny and interesting. But she did not dare to touch anything that lay within her father's perimeter.

Medraut fixed a date in the sling's cup and let it fly in one quick, smooth flick, without any windup and apparently without aiming at anything. In the arbor that shaded the south wall of the house, a ripe fig suddenly seemed to explode.

Medraut laid the sling in Telemakos's lap. Athena reached for it.

"Put it down," Telemakos told her, pulling the wrist loop in place with his teeth. Athena snatched at the sling, letting out little squeaks of possession and desire. The tail end trailed in the fish pool and got wet.

"Drop it," Medraut ordered darkly.

Athena instantly let go, like a scolded dog. Telemakos thought that Medraut could have said anything to her in that tone—"Eat up" or "Dancing time"—and she would have let go just as quickly.

Telemakos shook the water from the tail and laid open the cup between his fingers. It fell shut when he picked up a date. He tried again, and when he stood up to make the shot, the date fell out, dropping into the pool with a light *plip*. It floated, and Athena reached for it, then checked herself with a glance at Medraut and drew back.

Telemakos apologized. "I'm long out of practice."

"Give it me," Medraut said, but did not wait. He slipped the sling away from Telemakos. "Take three dates and hold them up to me one at a time."

Telemakos held one out. Medraut swung the empty sling and caught the date with it, shot into the tree, swung again, and caught the next date as Telemakos held it up. The woolen cord sizzled the tips of Telemakos's fingers as it whipped over them.

"Now let the child hold up a stone," Medraut ordered.

"She's afraid of you," Telemakos said. His fingers burned. "You'll hurt her."

"You take the sling, then. She'll hold one out for you. Here, child," Medraut said, his voice like silk, and serpentlike, gave Athena a date. She, seduced, took it in astonishment at her good fortune. She stared at Medraut with wide eyes like gray crystal. "Hold it for the boy. Up, like this. Now you, Telemakos, take the sling, let go the end—"

"I will not!" Telemakos raged at him. "I haven't the skill. I'll hit her! Mother of God! Are you mad? Tear up her trust in me for a silly thing like that? I won't do it!"

Athena turned her steady gray gaze from Medraut to Telemakos, and calmly put the date in her mouth.

Medraut drew in a ragged breath. Then he laughed.

"You are right, boy; I am touched with madness now and then."

Telemakos dared to glance upward at his father and saw that there was no malice in the storm-filled, dark blue eyes; Medraut was gazing at his daughter like a man watching a show of magic.

"You can teach her," Medraut said quietly. "Not yet, perhaps, but soon. She'll hold up the pellets for you. I'll fix a pocket on the saddle, so she can reach them. Practice taking them from me, to start with; it doesn't matter if you hit me. We won't hurt the little princess."

Telemakos pulled on the wrist loop again. He walked a few

paces away from Athena and practiced his cast. After a few attempts his body remembered what to do, but it would take a little longer for him to master the trick of catching up a stone held out to him halfway through the shot.

"If I learn to do this to your satisfaction, and can defend myself, can I go through the city unescorted?"

"Whenever have you needed to defend yourself walking through your own city?" Medraut asked.

"You said it would afford me protection."

"From hyenas, boy, not men." Medraut looked up at Telemakos, concern showing as anger in his cold gaze. "Whom do you fear?"

"I thought—" Telemakos had been housebound so long that he had begun to equate it with imprisonment.

"Before my accident—" Telemakos shaded the truth a little, to protect Goewin as his source. "When I used to go up to the New Palace for my lessons, I heard some talk of omens and the emperor's servants being menaced and evildoers unaccounted for. Some of it was aimed at me, or anyway at what I was last year, and I thought that if it had happened recently, you would want me under guard."

Medraut was silent.

"I'm not afraid of walking in the street alone," Telemakos said. "Only I thought you might not let me."

"No one knows what you were last year. Believe me, we watch for it, the certain threat." Medraut went back to his stitching and spoke as he worked. "But it has been a quiet year, even for Goewin. Everyone knows the quarantine is to be lifted at winter's end. That gives people hope, honest men and evildoers alike. You're safe enough in the street.

"When I've finished," Medraut added, "you may take the baby up to the New Palace and show her your lions at last, if you like. Sheba is expecting kits."

Solomon remembered Telemakos as a friend, not as dinner. The big lion stood at the bottom of the lion pit looking lonely and bewildered, gazing longingly up at the viewing terrace and purring loud, leonine invitations in Telemakos's direction.

Athena loved the lions. She growled and chirruped so convincingly she confused them. She could imitate birdsong, too, and the clucking of chickens, and all the range of noises made by Grandfather's horses. She had more animal noises than she did human words.

"What do you suppose Solomon's saying, little owlet? 'Why do you never play with me anymore, boy?'"

"Telemakos Meder!"

Telemakos heard light footsteps on the flagstone stair that led up to the terrace garden. It was a woman's voice that called his name; for a moment he could not place it.

"Or shall I call you Beloved Telemakos, the lionhearted, as the emperor does always now? Boy, you are never about when I look for you. How I have missed your company this past year!"

It was Sofya Anbessa, the emperor's youngest cousin. She leaped up the stairs three at a time, clutching her skirts about her knees, hurrying as though she expected Telemakos to vanish before she got there.

Athena reached for Telemakos's hair, a thing she did for reassurance. She was uncertain of strangers. Telemakos said coolly, "You cannot have looked very hard. Did you try Counselor Kidane's mansion? I have my own bedroom there—"

Sofya stopped his mouth by laying her hand across it.

"Don't ever."

She tapped his lips sharply with her fingertips.

"Never doubt my faith. I have been to hell and back on your account."

She had brought him out of Afar. She was three years older than Telemakos, which meant that she was old enough to marry, while he was still younger than the newest of Gebre Meskal's guard. Telemakos felt this difference to be vaster now than it had been two years ago, when she had bought his freedom from the salt pirates.

"They have taken me off studying South Arabian and put me on Latin," Sofya went on. "I am shut in half the day with my Latin tutor, and half with the royal cartographer, and if it were possible, I think yet another half with your aunt, learning how Constantine the high king of Britain and Cynric the king of the West Saxons have carved up your foreign grandfather's kingdom between them. In any case, Ras Meder never allowed a soul into the House of Nebir to see you when you were ill. I tried for a month. He would not let the *emperor* in."

"I was here in the New Palace for the first month—"

Telemakos began, speaking through Sofya's fingers. Athena pulled Sofya's hand away. "Thank you, Athena," Telemakos said. "I said, I was here, in this palace—"

"So was I. I sat by your side every evening for a fortnight and listened to you wailing to go home. Then they began to carve collops out of you, and I was not let in again."

Telemakos had no memory of her being there at all.

"Oh," he said. "Well. Perhaps you did."

Athena still had hold of Sofya, and Sofya shook her hand a little without actually making her let go. "Sweet heart, little owlet, do you remember your auntie Sofya? Mmm? Was it not I who first bought you honey and almond paste, at the confectioners' fair, when your tight-fisted British aunt said it would rot your six new teeth? Have you added to the six yet? Let me see."

Athena dropped Sofya's fingers and pressed her face into Telemakos's shoulder.

"Aye, that is what my twin sister always did if anyone spoke to her, before she was married. She always tried to hide herself in my dress. Except she was a deal bigger than you, so it was more annoying."

"My mother clings to my clothes as well, lately," Telemakos said wryly. "She doesn't believe I'll stay out of the lion pit just because Nezana keeps the tunnel locked."

"He has taken away the rope, too," Sofya observed, climbing onto the stone bench to kneel backward and look down at Solomon pacing below. "As if you might—" She hesitated.

"—suddenly sprout a new arm," Telemakos finished for her.

Sofya coughed, then snickered, and presently they both dissolved in hysterical, choking laughter.

Then Athena growled. It was a lion noise, not an angry noise; Telemakos had moved away from the railing, and she could no longer see the lions. He climbed up to kneel beside Sofya, bracing Athena between them against the back of the bench.

"Have you seen the kits?" Sofya asked. "Sheba scarcely ever brings them out."

"I've only been up here a little while, but she hasn't moved. I keep hoping. Nezana says she won't suckle them, or doesn't let them suckle, or is just stupid. He's waiting for her to leave them alone so he can bring them away from her."

Athena reached out to pull at the ropes of emerald that were always plaited into Sofya's hair. The princess expertly twitched the baby's hand away.

"Tena," Athena said, grabbing at the emeralds again. Sofya sat back on her heels, facing the baby.

"Tena, my love, it is a clever girl that knows her own name," Sofya said. "You must learn to say Sofya, next. Sofya."

"Sofya," Athena repeated obediently.

"You little vixen!" Telemakos exclaimed. "What's my name, then? Who's this?" He tapped himself on the chest.

Athena identified him lovingly. "Boy."

Sofya laughed. "Telemakos is too long, isn't it? Silly, pompous Greek name."

"Thank you. Why are you learning Latin and the names of British kings?" Telemakos asked.

Sofya coughed again. She arranged her skirts around her knees. She seemed uncharacteristically apologetic when she spoke.

"I am to go to Britain in the summer, when the rains and the quarantine are over, as the new ambassador there. I shall be counterpart to your aunt Goewin."

Telemakos felt a stab of envy at the thought of the adult assignment that lay ahead of her, representing her kingdom in formal embassy to a distant and important ally. That Gebre Meskal should choose a girl as his ambassador—Goewin surely had a hand in this recommendation.

"Does that mean your brother Priamos is coming home?" Telemakos asked. "Goewin will be pleased."

"If he is still alive, after the plague, yes."

"I shall miss you."

"Rot. You have not missed me all this year."

"Tena! My my my my my!"

Athena reached for Sofya's hair again, and Sofya began to pick absently at one of her long plaits, twisting a glinting rope of green jewels from her hair. She held it out to Athena, who tried to tangle it into her own wild bronze curls. When she found the beads would not stay on her head, she put them in her mouth.

"What kind of baby are you, that teethes on emeralds?" Sofya said, wrapping the tail end of the string about her hand so that Athena could not accidentally swallow it. "Do not fall into one of your black sulks, Telemakos so-called lionheart; you look like your father. It is very unbecoming. You are not ambassador to Britain yet, but you can be sure the emperor has plans for you as well."

She stretched out the emeralds. Athena growled, a warning growl this time, and kept on chewing. "These jewels I wear all belonged to my father," Sofya went on. "And so did those my mother the queen of queens gave you, last year."

"What are you talking about?"

"The emerald collar you wore at the smugglers' trial. The queen of queens did an odd thing when she gave that collar to you. She should have given it to one of her sons. But my eldest brother, Mikael, is mad insane and imprisoned, and the next, Abreha, is king of Himyar and will not come back to Aksum; and Hector is dead; and Priamos is in Britain. So she gave it to you. And that is sort of like adopting you as her son. It does an odd thing for you; so long as Gebre Meskal has no sons of his own, it puts you in favor to be chosen as his heir."

Telemakos gave a disbelieving snort. "That's as likely as the sprouting of a new arm!"

"You're not his blood kin," Sofya said, and her face was serious now. "But you are heir to the house of Nebir, and you have the unspoken endorsement of the queen of queens. All her own sons are useless or dangerous. Do you see? It makes you a favorite, *Beloved* Telemakos. 'Beloved' is a *title*. Did you think it was an endearment?"

This was, in its own way, as chilling as any hyena's head in the palace kitchens.

"I had not thought about it," Telemakos said faintly.

"It was my father's title," said Sofya. "Ras Bitwoded Anbessa, the beloved prince Lionheart. When the emperor calls you 'Beloved Lionheart' it puts everyone in mind of my father, who was chief counselor to the emperor Caleb, before Gebre Meskal was born.

"Ah me," she added caustically. "I am sorry to make you have to think so hard."

Telemakos, used to her insults, glared fixedly down at Solomon. "Well, I see now why no one will let me touch a spear. I might perhaps arrange a royal hunt, go kill a lion and prove myself a worthy rival to the kingship, and have to be imprisoned somewhere."

"You look like Ras Meder again," Sofya said. "Your sister will think it is acceptable behavior to scowl at anyone who tries to instruct you—"

"Oh!" Telemakos gasped in sudden delight. *"There they are!"*

The lioness Sheba had paced away to stretch. The three cubs had been sleeping close against her, curled together in an intertwining ball of golden fluff. Telemakos had never seen lions so small and new.

"Look, look, Tena," he whispered, gazing at them in rapture, and it was only after Sheba had come back and sat on them again, as though they were eggs in a nest, that Telemakos realized Sofya had been watching him all the while through narrowed eyes, as intent on him as he had been on the lion cubs.

"It is true that I have missed your company," she said softly. "I am sorry to be going away in such a little while."

Two of Sheba's babies died within a week of their birth. Telemakos was in agony over the state of the remaining kit, until the morning Nezana called at Grandfather's gate with the thin, faintly breathing scrap of fur sleeping in a basket.

"The emperor Gebre Meskal asks if Telemakos Meder will raise this cub for him," the lion keeper requested formally. "There is no one better able to manage such a task."

"I should like a word with the emperor Gebre Meskal," Medraut told him in the silken serpent's voice that made you want to run and hide.

But Grandfather unexpectedly threw in his support with Telemakos. They stood in the courtyard arguing while the lion, scarcely old enough to blink, lay quietly starving in its basket.

"I would not care if Gebre Meskal were emperor of Rome," Medraut said coldly. "He will ask my permission before he offers my son so mocking and dangerous a gift."

"He has already asked my permission," Grandfather said gruffly, "and the child is my heir. It is not a gift, and it is only for a short time, to save the creature's life. If the cub lives, Gebre Meskal will send it to Himyar when the quarantine ends, as a token of esteem to his cousin the king Abreha

Anbessa. It will be gone from here before it drops its milk teeth."

Medraut capitulated ungraciously.

"It had better be."

He and Telemakos made a bed for it in an empty stall of Kidane's stables.

"When you were trod on by a stag and broke every bone in your body, and smashed your hand to splinters, no one stopped you going hunting again," Telemakos pointed out to his father.

"I was more than twice your age. I made my own decisions."

"But you must have been more careful afterward. Didn't it change the way you hunt? I'll never make my great mistake twice."

Medraut sighed. He answered wryly, "In truth, I took no lesson from it at all. So you are already in advance of me."

"It's only a little lion," Telemakos assured him.

They called it Menelik, after the son of King Solomon and the queen of Sheba.

It was such a loving and doglike creature that it was soon allowed to roam about the villa as it pleased. Watching the lion, Athena began to walk on all fours, like a cat, instead of crawling. Legs splayed slightly to keep her body level, she scampered about the house in a sort of intermediate step between crawling and walking. She was very fast.

She was like Menelik in other ways too. You could amuse them both, easily, with the same bells and balls and bits of string. They played a game together in which Athena sat on a small rug in the lobby, calling to the young lion in perfect imitation of his own soft chirps, until Menelik came pelting through the reception hall to throw himself onto the rug. Then they would both go skidding across the floor in a tangle of wool and fur and springing uncombed hair. A good deal of Telemakos's winter was spent in retrieving the carpet. Their mother played, too, calling to Menelik, spreading the carpet out for them, helping to untangle Athena.

Medraut did not play. He sat quietly, with his knees drawn up to his chest, keeping an eye on the lion. And he watched Turunesh. Telemakos thought he looked hungry, watching her, as though he were feeding on her laughter.

She still seemed tired, but she was no longer half asleep.

One night toward winter's end, Medraut came into the house late from some errand and found his children and wife and sister and Menelik all asleep in the sitting room, where Goewin had been reading aloud to them, with the oil lamp still wastefully burning. Medraut woke them, tossed the sleeping baby carelessly over his shoulder, and ushered Telemakos to bed, scolding him all the while for leaving the lion loose.

"There you are, princess," Medraut said to Athena, putting her down gently in a corner of Telemakos's bed. "Keep your brother company so he doesn't wake us all with his evil dreams."

Telemakos leaned his cheek against her round, warm back and took a deep breath of her odd, dry-forest-floor baby smell.

If I had not had my accident, Telemakos thought, I would not have had so much time or attention to spend on Athena, and maybe she would not love me as she does. And I would give my soul to have her love. I would give my soul to save her life. Maybe my arm was a small sacrifice.

A year ago, he thought, exactly a year ago, I was *dying.* Surely the worst is past me now.

VII

The Gates Thrown Wide

SUMMER CAME EARLY. Bright yellow highland asters flooded the banks of Mai Barea. The fields above the city were so thick with them that the New Palace seemed to float in an ocean of gold. Telemakos went out, with Athena riding in her harness and the small lion trotting at the end of a lead ahead of them. Last year at this time, Telemakos had been in bed, and the year before that, in the coastal city of Adulis, so it was three years since he had seen the Meskal daisies in bloom.

The highways teemed with traffic, for the quarantine was over. It had been lifted when the rains ended, three weeks before the new year began. Telemakos took Athena to the Avenue of Thrones, where children and beggared veterans watched an unfamiliar and astonishing parade of foreigners and foreign goods arriving in the city. Gedar's two younger boys were there, waiting anxiously for their father.

"Come and let your sister try her teeth on this!"

"Eon! Eon!" Athena cried. She knew all the neighbors' names, though she still would or could not say "Telemakos."

You Jezebel, thought Telemakos jealously, and joined the neighbors' children where they sat on the highest step of the platform supporting one of the ceremonial granite thrones. Japheth and Eon were so smitten with Athena that Telemakos was forced to forgive them their traditional rivalries. Telemakos found Japheth to be grudgeless and generous and a useful source of information.

"Big brother Sabarat's given me spending money," Japheth said. "He guides the spice merchants to the markets and helps them find lodging." He lifted a handful of toasted kolo grain from a sack and let it trickle back through his fingers. "Have some!"

In this way Telemakos was the first of Kidane's household to know when Gedar came home at the start of the new year, wearing an embroidered shamma of finely woven cotton and leading a laden mule. The mule's burden included two sacks of mail directed to various members of the house of Nebir.

Grandfather and Goewin sorted through their mail together in the reception hall. Goewin sat on the floor amid a sea of parchment, tearing open letters with unsteady hands, sobbing and chuckling and scrubbing absently at tears. Grandfather's letter opening was more sober; he worked at a writing table and filed his receipts into baskets.

"What's all this?" Telemakos asked, unbuckling the straps that held Athena's saddle at his side. He knelt and let Athena climb out of her harness. She moved nimbly, her arms and legs smooth and slender. She had never been chubby; at just over one year old, she already looked like a small girl rather than a baby.

"Mercy on us, *not* in the middle of the post!"

Telemakos snatched Athena up again. She might be a small girl, but she was getting big for him to lift easily. She reached for the palm scrolls and crackling parchment, bright with seals and ribbons.

"Here, have these," Goewin said, sifting through documents to find something she could spare. "Rubbish."

"Why are you crying?"

"Priamos wrote to me every week during the quarantine. *Every week.*" They had not seen Priamos Anbessa for seven years. Priamos was the emperor's cousin and Sofya's older brother, the Aksumite ambassador to Britain. Telemakos remembered him as kind and frowning, a gentle, humorous man with an unaccountably angry face. Goewin had no dearer friend.

"In the beginning he wrote every two or three days," Goewin said. "I think there must be two hundred letters here."

"Is he all right?"

"As of last season. There's nothing less than three months old. Look, Telemakos, my love, he's sent a letter to you as well."

Telemakos could not take it because he was still reining Athena back. She reached for the letter.

"Sit on my knee then, Tena. Here, I'll open it and you can hold it while I read."

"Goodness, you're training her well."

"She's harder work than the lion, I can tell you."

Telemakos read slowly, shaping the words silently with his lips.

"They're all alive!" he said joyfully.

"Well, the high king and his Comrades are alive. Listen to Constantine's tale."

Telemakos sat folding his letter for Athena to unfold, as Goewin pieced together for him Britain's own story of quarantine and plague. Page after page gave up a harrowing account of the high king Constantine's four-month self-imposed imprisonment on his island fortress in Dumnonia.

"Half of Britain is destroyed," Goewin finished grimly, picking up another letter. "But Constantine has saved himself and his court. He did not save his wife and two young children. I do not know if I could have been so ruthless."

"Don't speak nonsense, Princess," Kidane said mildly, cutting the twine around a minute wicker hamper handed him by Ferem, who waited on him. "What of the ruin of our port city Deire, when plague was there and the emperor's soldiers were ordered to shoot flaming arrows into anyone who tried to escape?"

"I did not advise that."

"You sanctioned it."

"So did you, Councilor Kidane, though you may call me heartless." Goewin spoke fiercely, defending herself.

She broke the seal on the letter she held. Grandfather

opened the lid of his parcel. Ferem, who could see over Kidane's shoulder, reached to take back the box, but Grandfather held up a hand to stay him.

"You should look at this, Goewin Dragon's Daughter," Kidane said quietly. "Look quickly, for I do not want to keep it here."

She glanced up from her letter. "What is it?"

"A warning has come."

Goewin carefully moved the pile of letters from her lap onto the floor and got to her feet. "What warning? To whom?" she asked in a low voice.

"The box is addressed to me," Kidane said evenly, "but it is my house, of course."

Goewin leaned over the table as Kidane pushed the parcel toward her. She picked up the box and lifted the lid. After a moment she narrowed her eyes and sneered in disturbed disgust, then suddenly slammed the lid shut. Telemakos saw all the color drain from her face as if a white person's cheeks were a cup from which the blood could be poured out.

"This is a death threat," Goewin whispered. "Who sent it?"

"I don't know," Grandfather answered with more ragged frustration in his voice than Telemakos had ever heard from him. "Who sends any of them? *I don't know.*"

"What is it?" Telemakos asked, letting Athena go. She pulled herself up against Grandfather's desk and helped herself to one of the documents lying there. She dropped it on the floor and reached for another, but no one stopped her.

Grandfather turned his face toward Telemakos with a furrow of concern drawing his brows together. Goewin followed Kidane's gaze, her eyes wide with shock and her lips parted as though she were about to speak. Quickly she looked down at the box in her hands, then dropped it on the writing table as though it burned her fingers. Telemakos scrambled to his feet and reached for it himself, but Goewin snatched it up again.

"Do not."

Telemakos smelled dust and faint decay.

"What is it?" he repeated. "Let me see."

"*Do not,*" Grandfather echoed in sharp agreement.

Goewin's skirts swept through one of her careful piles of parchment. Holding the box beyond Telemakos's reach, she pounded out the front door and ran down the forecourt stair.

"Goewin!"

Telemakos left Athena among Priamos's two hundred letters and raced after his aunt. Goewin ran across the courtyard to the kitchen wing.

"Let me see!"

Goewin threw the thing into one of the brick ovens. Telemakos, unthinking, plunged after it. Goewin pulled him out of the flames and boxed his ears so forcefully she knocked him over.

He went down hard, flailing for balance. Illusion tore away his being. *My arms are bound, my hands are tied, I cannot see, I cannot see—*

He could not break his fall. He took the woodpile down

with him. The kitchen turned over, re-formed itself, and Telemakos saw Goewin snatch up a pair of kitchen tongs and rake coals over the little box. The wicker burst into flame; Goewin pounded the flaming parcel into ash.

Then she looked down at Telemakos. His eyes stung with smoke and fury and phantom salt.

"Forgive me, love," Goewin whispered, kneeling by his side. "Did I hurt you?"

Grandfather's cook was at his other side, bristling with outrage. "Get out of my kitchen!" she snapped at Goewin. "Such cockfighting ill becomes a pullet hen! Strike Telemakos Meder again and I'll break an oil jar over your foreigner's head. *Mother of God!* It is not a year since the child had his arm taken off, and you would beat him to the ground!"

Telemakos blinked fixedly, not daring to rub his burning eyes. Cook helped him to his feet and stirred the ashes.

"And what offal have you thrown on my fire?" she demanded.

"Just as you say. Offal. Worthless scrap." Goewin shook her head as though trying to clear it. "Come, Telemakos."

"Come back in an hour, boy, and I'll have honey cakes fried for you," the cook said.

"Don't cook anything on that fire," Goewin said, with icy command. "Sweep it out and build another. I shall send the houseboy to assist you." She held Telemakos close against her with one arm over his shoulder and the other around his waist, her hands clasped protectively over his galloping heart. "I vow there is good reason for everything I do," she said. Her voice was cold as frost, but her embrace was warm.

"Come away," she repeated in Telemakos's ear.

She let go of him, and they walked together soberly across the yard back toward the house.

"I'll tell Kidane to have the next post sent to his office in the New Palace," Goewin muttered, "and spare us all another such adventure."

"What was it?"

Goewin voice went cold once more. "Don't ask me again, Telemakos."

Telemakos abandoned Athena to his mother and her maid for most of the morning, a thing he never did, so that he could shadow his grandfather like a ghost. Kidane led him from reception hall to study, back for a few minutes to Turunesh's chamber and out to the garden, while Telemakos crept behind urns and wall hangings and potted palms, frantically hoping Kidane would drop some hint of what he and Goewin had seen in the little wicker box.

By afternoon Telemakos was exhausted by his own subterfuge. It was dull and nerve-racking all at once. How could I possibly have spent the first ten years of my life listening at doors? he wondered. There must be better ways to find out secrets.

He collected Athena and sat down with her on the wide dais in front of the house, rolling his mother's empty bobbins down the steps. Turunesh rarely used them now, and the reels made fragile towers for Athena to knock down, if you balanced them carefully. Telemakos thought he could use this game to teach Athena to climb the stairs, but she refused to cooperate: she let Menelik fetch the bobbins for her.

She was sitting at the top of the stair and Telemakos at the bottom when the emperor Gebre Meskal himself walked across the forecourt, carrying in one hand a box identical to the one Goewin had thrown into the kitchen fire.

Telemakos went cold, then hot.

The emperor wore his customary plain white kilt and shamma, and the head cloth of gold-shot linen that was the mark of his sovereignty. His two ceremonial spear bearers stood at his back. Telemakos lay full length on the ground at the emperor's feet, as his grandfather had taught him.

"Beloved Telemakos," Gebre Meskal said, his firm voice gentle, "my young lion. You need not stand on ceremony in the privacy of your grandfather's house. Come to your feet." He knelt by Telemakos and held forth an open palm, which Telemakos took hesitantly. The emperor's narrow hand was warm and dry, with a stern grip. Gebre Meskal raised Telemakos to his feet and released him.

"What game are you playing?" Gebre Meskal knelt again, and picked up a bobbin.

"We're idling," Telemakos answered. His attention, but not his gaze, was riveted on the box that the emperor held in his other hand. "Throw again, Athena. Show the emperor how his lion can fetch."

She picked up a spindle in each hand and hurled them

down the stairs. There was no force, no coordination, no aim behind her pitch, and the reels clattered slowly from granite step to granite step. One rolled on toward the spear bearers' feet. The nearest guard batted at the reel with the butt end of his spear, pushing it teasingly just beyond Menelik's reach, and the little lion chased wildly around his legs after it. The soldier laughed, and stamped his iron-strapped boots.

"Boy!" Athena wailed, startled by the noise. "Tena boy up—" In a panic to be close to Telemakos, she tried to climb down the stairs.

Telemakos had coached her well enough that she had the sense to turn around and make her way feetfirst. But then she could not see where she was going or where Telemakos was. Halfway down she stopped and wailed again pathetically, "Boy! Tena! Boy!" Telemakos vaulted up the steps and sat down beside her. She tried to climb into his lap.

"I can't hold you on the stairs, Tena; be still."

She stood tight against his side, clutching his hair.

"Sit down," he hissed, embarrassed at all this to-do in front of Gebre Meskal. He managed to get her to release his head.

Gebre Meskal set down the bobbin, and his box, on the step below Athena.

"She calls you 'Boy'?"

"It's better than 'Mama,' which is what she calls Goewin and the maids and the cook and even poor Ferem. Any old body who takes care of her is 'Mama.' 'Boy' is special."

Telemakos leaned forward and took a deep breath. The

emperor's package gave off the same faint dusty smell as Kidane's had.

"What does she call her father?"

"Ras. Prince."

The emperor nodded. "Of course." Then he said to Athena directly, "What a pretty bracelet!" She shrank back, hiding her wrist between herself and Telemakos, gazing steadily at her sovereign with clear, solemn eyes. "Let me carry her in," Gebre Meskal offered.

Telemakos did not think he would have made such an offer to anyone with two arms and did not like to insult the emperor by declining it. But he was afraid Athena would scream and shame them all.

"Do you forgive me, Majesty, she is no trouble to me." Telemakos glanced over his shoulder. He had left her harness at the top of the stair. "Come on, Athena," he said. "Up to your saddle, and I'll carry you."

"Let me get it for you," said Gebre Meskal mildly.

He climbed the stairs past Telemakos.

Telemakos acted without thought. With his knee he knocked down the bobbin the emperor had been holding. It fell to the bottom of the steps, where Menelik raced after it around the guards' feet again. For half a dozen seconds, the spear bearers were inattentive, and the emperor's back was turned.

"Open that box," Telemakos hissed in Athena's ear, through the shining bronze cloud of her hair.

She lifted the lid willingly. They peered in together.

Athena cheeped and warbled, which was her way of saying *bird.* Telemakos drew in a sharp breath.

"Shut it," he whispered.

His heart seemed to go cold and numb, the way it sometimes did in his dreams, as he lay bound and waiting to be tortured. *This is a death threat,* Goewin said.

Trapped by his own devious behavior, Telemakos now had to keep his face and voice perfectly composed as the spear bearers came to attention. He managed it. The emperor came down the stair with Athena's carrier, and waited while Telemakos put it on. Telemakos's fingers felt cold and numb, too.

Gebre Meskal picked up the evil little parcel and said seriously, "Is your aunt at home, Beloved One? I want to talk to her."

When Telemakos answered, his voice did not shake. He marveled at his own steady detachment. "She's in Grandfather's study, opening her mail. I'll take you in, Majesty."

Telemakos drew another deep breath. Even the air seemed cold. He pushed himself to his feet to escort the emperor and his guards upstairs, clutching Athena around the shoulder until she pushed him away in annoyance. Goewin firmly barred him from following them into Grandfather's study.

Telemakos went back outside and sat down again on the steps with Athena. He laid his cold cheek against his sister's burning bronze hair. She chirped, remembering the box and the bird it had contained.

"Sunbird," Telemakos whispered his second name into

her sandalwood-scented hair. "That was a sunbird."

The small wicker coffer had held a withered heap of iridescent green feathers. These had been carefully arranged, the long sweep of the tail teased to fit into the cramped space without bending or breaking. The shining body had a nail through its heart.

It was like a thing in a dream. It could not be real. Yet it burned against his vision, bright against the darkness, a murdered sunbird: the stud end of a nail lodged among the shining breast feathers, the point piercing out between the small shoulder blades, the carefully twisted tail.

VIII

A Shout in the Street

THEY TOLD HIM nothing. They told him that the house of Nebir was under threat, but that was nothing.

He was not allowed beyond the walls of Grandfather's villa. Goewin refused Kidane's suggestion of a warrior escort when she went out, but she took Medraut with her as her own personal bodyguard, and Medraut could knock arrows to his bow three at a time. It reminded Telemakos of the first year Goewin spent in Aksum, half his lifetime ago: for a time she had used him as her collateral because he was grandson to Britain's last high king, and no one had been allowed out of the house without a guard. They had not told him anything then, either.

A fortnight into the new year came the Feast of the Cross, Meskal, from which Gebre Meskal took his name as emperor. Hard upon the feast was the great parade in which the emperor's councilors and soldiers all pledged their service to their sovereign for another year. No formal pledge was required of

Telemakos, whose duty to the emperor was not spoken of in public. But Kidane had to be there, and Goewin. Medraut would not let his sister walk vulnerable and conspicuous across the Cathedral Square before the knowing eyes of the entire city, a strange and solitary woman among many men, making a bright and tempting target; nor would he leave Telemakos at home in an empty house. They were all to go.

Telemakos was torn between apprehension and wild relief at being allowed out of the house, even under guard, even to stand in the street for eight hours in formal dress. Mariam, his mother's favorite attendant, fought to tame his hair with wire combs and clarified butter. Telemakos sat clenching his teeth as she tied fast his head cloth. He had known he would have to wear it for this formal occasion and had been steeling himself. But Medraut must have spoken to Mariam beforehand; she was careful not to come near Telemakos's eyes. When she had finished, she turned him over to Ferem, who helped him into a shirt of brocaded linen and finally draped over Telemakos's shoulders the heavy collar of gold and emeralds that Sofya's mother, the queen of queens, had given him.

How many people in the Cathedral Square today will recognize this, Telemakos wondered; how many will know that it belonged to Ras Bitwoded Anbessa, the beloved prince Lionheart, and will they know that Gebre Meskal calls me Beloved, too? *A death threat.* How many know that he also calls me Sunbird?

He wished he did not have to wear the emeralds, or the head cloth.

His family was waiting for him in the forecourt. The morning sunlight on his shoulders was a shining bright green blur as Telemakos moved.

"You look grandson to Artos the Dragon this morning, Telemakos Meder!" Grandfather let slip in rare paternal pride. "An apt pretender to his line! What an honor that I harbor so many British princes!"

Medraut said curtly, "He owes nothing to Britain. He is Aksumite. And I do not like it that his emerald plumage glitters so."

"*Do you hush,*" Goewin snapped at them. "Will you shout hints for all the neighborhood to wonder at?"

Athena, who unlike Telemakos had not held quiet and unresisting while her hair was combed and oiled and beaded, was on the verge of emotional collapse by the time Telemakos made his appearance. She was angrily trying to pull her plaits out. She was also trying to pull her mother's plaits out, but saw Telemakos and lunged toward him.

"Oh!" Turunesh gasped, catching the baby before she dived headfirst out of the knotted cloth that she was tied up in.

Athena reached for Telemakos, shrieking and hissing like a cat. She made another attempt to throw herself backward out of her mother's arms.

"Let me take her, Mother. She'll calm down if she toys with

my hair. I'll use your carrying cloth, it'll save time. Help me settle her."

They had managed this exchange many times over the winter, but Telemakos's heavy clothes made him and his mother awkward this morning. "Under my mantle. The metal-work bites into my shoulders, pass the cloth underneath. Ai! Fix it *beneath*, Mother!"

"Let me help," said Goewin soothingly. The three of them managed together to fasten Athena against Telemakos's side.

"Boy's hair," Athena said, pulling at his head cloth with both hands.

"*Stop that*," he warned her sharply.

"Don't look," Goewin advised their mother, shepherding Turunesh toward the portal to the street. "He will use her as an excuse to get the head cloth off. I have never known your son to last in full finery for more than an hour."

Ferem pulled back the gate.

There was a splash of iridescent green marking the white limewashed cedar, as if someone had thrown a handful of emerald dye against it from the street.

Turunesh straightened her shoulders and stood still, gazing for a moment toward the quiet, sunlit avenue outside, then turning to Telemakos to gaze at him; and this seemed a natural connection, for the jewels over Telemakos's shoulders rippled with the same green light as the glinting thing in the entryway. As Telemakos looked at it again, the green blaze resolved itself into a small bird nailed to the gate.

The hair rose at the back of his neck.

"What in the name of God can be meant by this?" Turunesh hissed. With her own naked hands, she twisted the dead thing away from the gate and threw it into the street, and ground it underfoot with the heel of her slipper.

Telemakos shivered violently, as if he were stripped bare in Simien Mountain wind, instead of standing in sunlight in heavy clothes.

Athena warbled and then said, "Sunbird."

In sudden, irrational terror, Telemakos wrenched at Anbessa's gold collar until its links snapped in half a dozen places, and then he yanked the emeralds from his shoulders and ground them underfoot as his mother had done to the ragged feathers.

Athena raised her head in a piercing wail of pain and confusion. Gold wire had whipped her face as Telemakos had torn the collar off. There was a thin line of blood across her cheek. "Ai, sweet heart—" Telemakos gasped, all else forgotten, falling to one knee so he could bend to her more easily. Her hair in its neat woven rows gleamed like coils of new copper, and her skin glittered, too, where the tears streaked it. "Little owlet, your poor face—Let me see. . . ."

Goewin was at Telemakos's side, also trying to comfort Athena. Kidane and Ferem were in the avenue, Kidane scanning the empty street and Ferem kneeling over the remains of the bird as if it might tell him something. Medraut stood like a pillar of salt, silent, his look as bleak and wintry as if he had frozen to death in the instant of the gate's opening.

Turunesh suddenly seemed to pass fully from one world and into another. Her weariness was gone. She fired forth a barrage of instructions at Ferem, with cold command, like a queen.

"Bring me a basin of clean water. I want to wash my hands. Tell Ludim to sweep the street. Prise that nail out and have the gate scrubbed with salt."

She, too, knelt by Telemakos, and pulled her haunted, trembling son against her side. She folded both children in her arms at once; her voice was full of fear and misery and love. "Do you all think that because I have been unhappy I have become a simpleton? I will not keep my children any longer in this dreadful house."

The maligned house was so quiet that its silence woke Telemakos. He lay staring into the familiar dark for a while, then turned over with a sigh of frustration. Athena was at his side, asleep; he had not been dreaming. It seemed needless torment that along with all else he should now be lying awake.

After some time, as his eyes adjusted to the dark, Telemakos got up and went to look out the window. Yellow light shone faintly from a room two stories above his, Grandfather's bedchamber, perhaps. It was hard to tell in the dark, without being able to count windows. Maybe not Grandfather's room after all, because that was directly overhead. His study, then.

Telemakos went upstairs.

Goewin sat alone at Kidane's desk amid storage boxes and

documents. Before her lay all Telemakos's map-drawing tools and a pile of maps he had plotted that year. The one on top was the last he had made, showing the constellations of the zodiac. Telemakos had sketched lines connecting some of the stars to make pictures: the Lion, and the Scorpion. Goewin looked up at him, her face white and tear stained.

"Do you know what your grandfather said when we talked about it afterward? He said, 'It's time for that boy to be sequestered. We should have done it at his birth.' He wants to shut you away in the clifftop hermitage at Debra Damo, where they lock up all the lesser princes. And your father nodded and said it was a good idea."

Telemakos felt his throat close up. "For how long?" he croaked, and added, catching back a sob and not even waiting for her answer, "They put Priamos in chains when he was sequestered there, for disobedience. He was younger than me. Oh, Goewin, it will kill me if I am imprisoned again—it will *kill* me." He caught back another sob. "I will end up insane, like Mikael."

"I know. So I told them. Men are so stupid!" She blew out her breath explosively through pinched nostrils, a quick sound of irritated anger. "Your mother said we should send you to Himyar. And I thought that was a good idea, and between us we have overruled the men. You can study in San'a under Abreha's astronomer, which will raise no eyebrows at all, because Dawit Alta'ir is your uncle, your great-grandmother's brother. You have a British kinsman there as well, Medraut's foster brother Gwalchmei, my cousin. He is Constantine's ambassador in Himyar. Anyway, Abreha Anbessa owes me a favor. I helped him negotiate the peace that gave Himyar its independence from Aksum, and I appointed Gwalchmei. I am calling that to account.

"So." Goewin spoke determinedly in her fierce, steady way. "So. We are sending you to San'a in Himyar, to study with Dawit Alta'ir, Dawit the Eagle, the Star Master. You are going to apply yourself to maps and mathematics, and improve your South Arabian, and go hunting with those marvelous desert racing dogs Abreha keeps. I have written you a letter of recommendation, and the emperor will send one as well, and your excuse for going now will be that Abreha's little lion from Gebre Meskal needs an escort."

"What, I just *go*? On my own? I thought San'a was three weeks' trek into the Arabian mountains! Won't it take me half a season to get there? How did you make my father agree to that?"

"Abreha is in his port at al-Muza until Epiphany. Your father will take you as far as our own port in Adulis. You know you'll be safe with him; he'll travel by night and keep you away from the road if he has to. He'll put you on board one of your grandfather's merchant ships. When you arrive in Himyar, you'll take your recommendations and Abreha's lion and present yourself at the governor's mansion in al-Muza. Abreha will see you on to San'a."

Goewin rapped her fingers against a sealed letter that lay

alongside Telemakos's drawings and instruments. "We've made all ready. You'll leave tomorrow night."

"What are you doing with my things?"

"Packing them. What are you doing up here?"

Her white face was so pale she looked unearthly. Her eyes seemed depthless pools of black water, and the skin around them had a tight, bruised look to it.

"I think I heard you crying," Telemakos said. "I can't remember what woke me, but I think I must have heard you. And then I could not get back to sleep."

"I know how it is. I could not even make myself undress, the day that salt-doll thing was left on the doorstep. I sat awake all night long."

"Goewin, what happened to Hara?"

She turned over Telemakos's map. Beneath it lay another, the same constellations, with the Scorpion outlined and highlighted, and behind that lay another elaborate scorpion pricked out in stars.

"He fled Aksum with his final contraband load of salt," Goewin said, "so he may be alive and free somewhere, and perhaps he is now in this city, sending us a regular delivery of dead birds." She thumped a fist against Telemakos's maps. "Mother of God, Telemakos, I wish I knew."

"He wasn't really the kind of man who tried to frighten you," Telemakos said. "He just barked out orders to have you whipped if you did something wrong, and carried on with his own business. He wasn't as frightening as Anako. Anako liked to watch people being hurt."

Telemakos crossed the room and sat down at his aunt's feet, pressing close to her with his left side against her skirts. She laid one hand on his ruined shoulder, paging through his maps with the other.

"Maybe you should send me to Britain," Telemakos suggested, thinking with envy of Sofya. She, too, might have earned the hatred of the salt pirates, but as Britain's new Aksumite ambassador, she was already safe away while the dust cleared. "Grandfather said this morning that I am the long-lost heir to Artos the Dragon."

Goewin stopped his mouth with her hand. "That is not exactly what he said. You should treat that possibility as if it were as secret and dangerous as your work for the emperor. Never speak of it."

She tapped his lips in warning and took her hand away.

"Does Abreha know who I am—I mean, what I am?" Telemakos asked. "Are you going to tell him the real reason I am there?"

"You mean, will I tell him Gebre Meskal's spy needs a place to hide?"

Telemakos bowed his head. He bit nervously at the misshapen, rippling nails of his maimed fingers.

"Abreha does not know what you are," Goewin said. "The najashi, the king of Himyar, is a kind man, but I have never met a more manipulative political serpent. Abreha must never know what you are."

Telemakos said nothing, worrying the blunted nails.

"The emperor thinks these threats are not pointed at you," Goewin continued, and gently pulled Telemakos's fingers away from his mouth. "He thinks someone gleaned your name—not your real name, of course, but your secret name—as a code word from an intercepted message and is trying to use it to scare us without knowing its real meaning. It is outdated code, after all; two years have passed since you were in Afar. They may be trying to beat us out, to trick us into revealing ourselves." She paused. "They may think it is my name."

"They may think they can learn your name from me," Telemakos whispered. "They do in my dreams." He shuddered, his fingers at his mouth again.

"God forgive me," Goewin said, casting her face into her fists, with her elbows against Grandfather's desk. "I even figure in your nightmares." She pushed the papyrus leaves aside. Fanciful scorpions scattered over Telemakos's lap. "Just look at these."

"I should have done them in wax and rubbed them out after. They are a waste of paper."

"I have destroyed you," Goewin said.

Telemakos glanced over his shoulder at his aunt and saw her eyes brimming with tears again.

"Your father can blame Solomon, you can blame Hara or

Anako, but I blame no one but myself. I sent you to Afar. I knew what might happen if you were caught, and I sent you anyway. *Look at these.*"

She held up a scorpion of stars in either hand. On both sheets the star Antares, the scorpion's heart, was so fierce-ly drawn it pierced the pages through. Lamplight winked through one of the holes as Goewin put the pages down.

"You are enspelled, Telemakos. You are imprisoned under a dreadful sorcery that I myself have laid, and that I have no earthly power to undo. I'm confounded and damned if I know how to undo it."

Telemakos said nothing. He pressed a papyrus sheet beneath his foot and reached down to tear it carefully into strips.

"If the men who tormented you were dead," Goewin asked, watching Telemakos's slow destruction of the scorpion he had drawn, "would you rest easier?"

Telemakos rolled the shredded map into a ball.

"Please stop biting and tearing at things, Telemakos, it makes me want to tie you down. Look, here is something for you to fidget with. I have a present for you."

Goewin lowered an open case onto the floor at his feet. It held a bone cross-staff such as navigators use to work out the angles between stars.

"It's mine," Goewin said. "It was my mother's. Our steward sent it to me, with some of her things, when it was decided I would stay on in Aksum."

Telemakos ran his fingers along the finely etched marks across the staff's bone surfaces. The crosspiece slid smoothly, or could be fit into a series of minute notches. Telemakos lifted the staff from the box and held it carefully to his eye, as though he were sighting up the ceiling lamp. The instrument was light enough that he could hold it steady, but he could not hold it up one-handed and also slide the crosspiece. He set it down.

Goewin closed the cross-staff inside its case and laid it in the open box on the desk, alongside Telemakos's rules and stylus.

"You are good at keeping yourself inconspicuous," she said. "But your veins run with the blood of kings, and your mind is filled with the secrets of an empire. You are like a lamp burning quietly by itself in a dark room. Sooner or later someone is going to exploit your radiance . . ."

Her words trailed off.

". . . again," she finished softly.

Telemakos got to his knees and knelt before his aunt. She turned to face him. "Will you write to me?" Telemakos asked.

"Every week," Goewin promised. "As Priamos does to me."

She pressed her fingertips against his chest.

"You said once that I am your Mentor, your Athena. I wish I was, Telemakos; I wish I could give you the protection of a goddess, and watch over you disguised as a bird or an old man, and magically turn aside the blows aimed at you. But all I can do is wait and hope, like a mother who sees her sons off to war. Wait and hope, as I did while they took your arm off. I held my hand over your heart all through that final morning, so I could warn the surgeons of its faltering."

"Did it falter?"

"Not once." She laid her firm hand over his heart again, to show how she had done it. "Nor will it falter now. Fly free, my brave one, my sunbird. Take back the sky. Do not be afraid."

IX

THE HANISH ISLANDS

AS THEY LOADED the pack mules for the overland journey to Adulis, Medraut did something Telemakos could not remember ever having seen him do. He took Turunesh's hands and held them pressed between his own, gently, gently.

"You want them both to go." Medraut's voice was quiet. "Are you sure?"

"It will undo a year's healing to part them."

Medraut nodded. He still held Turunesh's hands in his. Her shoulders shook. She drew breath and drew herself up.

"I know I cannot go on with them to Himyar. What mother comes along to dote on her son in his first apprenticeship? But I can see him safely away," Turunesh said levelly. "I have business in Adulis. My uncle is archon there. Telemakos and I have stayed in the governor's house before. If we travel as a family, we will be less likely to draw attention to the child's escape."

The journey down the switchback mountain roads should

have taken a fortnight from Aksum; at the punishing pace Medraut set, they made Adulis in ten days. Turunesh and Telemakos took it in turns to carry Athena. They stopped by day away from the road, or by night in the homes of people Turunesh knew. No one troubled them.

In the hour before Telemakos left Adulis, Medraut stood with Telemakos on the scorching quay at Gabaza Harbor, resting his hands on his son's shoulders, and went one final time through his farewell litany.

"You are not to uncage that lion while you are on the ship. You must keep it on a lead until it is in Abreha's hands. And should you—should your shoulder trouble you, there is opium in the locked coffer with your allowances and recommendations. I have written to Abreha myself about the opium, for I do not trust you to use it at need." Medraut held Telemakos at arm's length, gazing at him searchingly, his hard, drawn face shadowed by a pained mix of love and fear. Telemakos lowered his eyes in respect.

"You know how to administer the opium," his father said.

"I've no need for opium."

"Then keep it carefully, you stubborn young ascetic," Medraut said. "Perhaps the need will come in another guise."

He raised his head and gazed toward Turunesh, who stood speaking to the ship's master with Athena tied to her hip. Her face, too, was lined with strain. Medraut looked away from her, wincing. He held his son's jaw cupped between his hard hands and kissed Telemakos on the forehead.

Turunesh took Telemakos on board, and the crew left them alone in the narrow sleeping bay below the deck to bid good-bye to each other. Athena, riding at her mother's side, looked about her with interest. There was no room to stand upright, so Turunesh sat cross-legged on the floor of the hold and patted the planking beside her in an invitation to her son to join her there. He nestled lovingly against her side opposite Athena.

"Telemakos, my love," Turunesh began, and stopped. She sucked in a choking breath and began over again: "Telemakos—"

He caught his mother's hand and held it against his cheek. Turunesh did not weep aloud, but tears began to leak from the corners of her eyes. Her other hand, the one he was not clinging to, combed absently through Athena's curls. Turunesh swallowed, and spoke in a low voice.

"Child, if you should ever need to tell us any private thing while you are in Himyar—I mean, anything concerning your service to the emperor, and the threats that have been made against you—do not confide in anyone there, even Abreha. And never write directly to Goewin of such things. Hide your secrets in a letter to me. Tell me that you send your love to your aunt, and encode your meaning in the sentences directly following your greeting to her. When you do this, we'll know that we must give our deepest attention to the message you send in that letter. Do you understand?"

"I think so," Telemakos whispered. Athena pulled at their clasped hands, trying to join in the embrace.

"You must never lie to Abreha. Do you understand?"

"I won't," said Telemakos. He was looking forward less and less to presenting himself to the king of Himyar, whom Goewin had called a manipulative serpent.

Turunesh smiled faintly. "You look like your father when he is about to wield his surgeon's knife, so grim and determined. Don't be afraid. Abreha the najashi has made his court a home to any noble child whose family was taken by plague. His own children are dead, all of them, the older ones he had by his first queen and the little ones he had by his new queen. Poor man, he is fond of children. Remember his kindness to you when he met Gebre Meskal to negotiate their peace?"

Abreha had indulged him, Telemakos recalled, but so had Solomon, before he tried to eat him.

"Abreha was my father's equal in the hunt," Telemakos said. "He looked like Priamos, but when he took Solomon from me, the day I caught the emperor's lions, he reminded me of Ras Meder." Telemakos paused, dredging for his earliest memories of the Aksumite imperial court. "When Aksum was at war with Himyar, he defeated Priamos in battle and sent him home unscathed."

"Yes. Abreha is like your father. He is a greater man than your father. He would seek justice where your father would seek revenge."

Gently, she began to untie Athena. Released, the baby climbed into Telemakos's lap, butting the top of her head affectionately against his chin the way the young lion did when it wanted attention.

"Here's the satchel. There is another gown for the baby, and clean napkins, and her goatskin bottle, and the painted animals my grandfather made for you when you were born."

The sounds of the harbor reached in to them, but dulled: the lap of water against the ship's hull, the cry of seabirds, the rumble of carts and shouts of men. "Up," Athena demanded of Telemakos, standing on his leg and pushing the shoulder strap of the harness Medraut had made for her against his neck. "Tena up."

"She is so like you," Turunesh said to Telemakos, holding Athena back as he put the sling on. "I look at her when she's asleep, with her fists behind her head and her lips just parted, and it is like seeing you a baby again, with those curling white lashes in a face like honey wine. Ah, Telemakos Meder, you have been my soul's joy these thirteen years. Shall I know you again when you return, striving toward manhood?"

Athena was content, as always, riding at Telemakos's side. It did not occur to her to miss her mother as they set out. She was interested in everything: the boat that towed their ship from the harbor, the sails unfurled, turtles in the water. She sat in the lion's crate, cuddling with Menelik; the ship's master gave her a dozen small pieces of ivory to sort and play with. She ate happily what was available, mango and dried fish that Telemakos had to pick the bones out of with his teeth before he dared give it to her. As dark fell, Telemakos let her stand balanced on a coil of rope looking for flying fish skimming the open sea beyond the Gulf of Adulis. She watched the sparkling water with incredible patience, waiting for the fish to surface, and shrieked with surprise and delight when they did. She showed no sign of weariness.

Close to midnight Telemakos judged her to have used up all possible energy and good nature. He tried to settle her in the sleeping bay.

"Milk," she said.

When she was tired, she wanted milk for comfort, even if it was only taken out of the goatskin.

"There isn't any milk on the boat, Tena. Suck your fingers. Here they are—"

She pushed them away disdainfully.

"Have mine, then."

That worked for about thirty seconds.

"Milk!"

"Hush, let's rock awhile," Telemakos whispered. So they did, for a few minutes, but now her clothes were damp again and she was uncomfortable, and she had not forgotten that she wanted milk.

"She'll be happier on deck," came the voice of one of the off-duty sailors beside them in the dark.

That meant, *Some of us are trying to sleep down here. Go away.*

Telemakos coaxed Athena in the direction of the cargo hold. She could not yet walk; she still went on all fours to get about. Telemakos was not certain enough of his footing on board the ship to dare to carry her without fixing her in her saddle. He went on his knees alongside her as she crept forward on hands and feet, stopping every yard or so to sit down on her sagging rump and insist, with growing urgency, "Milk. Tena's *milk*."

The cargo hold was packed with elephant tusks, some tightly roped together, others stacked behind wooden slats fixed in the ribs of the ship's hull. Telemakos found a place to wedge himself between the bundles.

"Come sit here."

She did not want to sit. She pulled herself up to stand against a sheaf of tusks and looked around.

"Wet," she said.

He could have kicked himself when he realized he had left her fresh clothes at the other end of the ship. He was steadily falling prey to a faint, unrelenting seasickness and could not face the toiling journey back to get her satchel. He swore he would never become a navigator, nor ever again be responsible for keeping a baby clean.

Telemakos stripped off Athena's pungent, clammy linens and swaddled her in his shamma. He had to keep snatching hold of her to prevent her trying to climb over the mountains of ivory. She was without direction but determined.

"Stay still, or I will throw you overboard! Do you want to go live among the sea turtles?"

She burst into fresh tears. "Bed," she sobbed, changing her tactics. "Tena's bed."

"There is only my blanket, back where the sailors are sleeping, and you can only go there if you *stop crying for milk!*"

When the night was half done, Athena cried herself to sleep at last, despite no milk, with her head pressed hard against Telemakos's breastbone and both hands tangled in his hair. She slept so lightly that when he tried to take her hands away, she struggled and wept. So he dozed, imprisoned, his head bent to Athena's grip, his body caged by the cargo of ivory.

By the next midday, Athena had used up all her clean clothes, and she flatly refused to be tied into a piece of sail-cloth. Telemakos considered this battle before engaging in it. He would not want his private parts bound up in thick canvas, either. Athena's clear gray eyes glinted with intelligence and misery as he spoke to her.

"You do not have to wear it," Telemakos said. "But this is what you have to do instead. You know what the lion does?"

For three days Athena scrambled about the deck without a stitch on, enviably indifferent to the ship's motion. Her fair bronze skin burned in the sweltering Red Sea glare, and by the third day even the threat of the sailcloth was enough to set her screaming in outrage and fury. By the fourth day she managed on her own, as efficient as Menelik, sharing the lion's earth box.

Telemakos did not sleep much during the voyage. The nausea kept him awake when Athena did not, and he grew irritable and nervous. He worried about the lion, moping limply in its cage. He tried, and failed, to mend a buckle that was coming loose on Athena's harness. He practiced with his sling, aiming at the flying fish that sometimes shot like silver darts through the foam alongside the ship, then felt sorry when he accidentally hit one. He longed to have the voyage over, and to be past the first meeting with Abreha Anbessa.

On the afternoon of the fifth day at sea, the blue horizon was suddenly stabbed by two sharp mountain crags, menacing as the towering peaks of thunder clouds.

"The taller peak is Zuqar Island, and the lesser Hanish al-Kabir," the ship's master told Telemakos. "The black sentinels of the Hanish Archipelago."

Telemakos stared at the twin volcanic heights, matching their silhouettes with the familiar outlines he remembered from Goewin's maps.

"Rich pearl-fishing grounds, there," the master said, "and a breeding ground for piracy. Zuqar is a traders' outpost, where goods exchanged go free of the duty they would be subject to in Aksum or Himyar. The other islet, Hanish al-Kabir, is Gebre Meskal's prison of exile."

The master followed Telemakos's gaze toward the ominous mountains. "Long ago, evildoers were abandoned on al-Kabir without water. Now there is a cistern and a properly adminis-trated prison. They quarry obsidian and eat shellfish."

Anako is there, Telemakos thought, if he is still alive. I sentenced him to exile. Is he on Hanish al-Kabir now, endur-ing a barren life of stonecutting and thirst? Maybe he dreams he's watching someone hammer a nail through my heart, the way I dream he is ordering Hara to do it.

◆　◆　◆

The next afternoon they were in the Himyar port of al-Muza. Telemakos stood on the white coral beach there, with Athena belted to his hip, and leaned down to peer into Menelik's crate. His stomach swooped. After six days at sea, his sense of balance had once more been knocked awry; he caught himself on his knees to avoid falling on his face.

Athena clutched frantically at her brother's shoulder. Her saddle was not as secure as it should be, because the slipping buckle still needed mending. Telemakos gripped the strap with his teeth and pulled hard to tighten it, then leaned close to the slats of the lion's hutch to look at Menelik.

It was sweltering inside. The young lion, highland bred, lay curled against the wooden staves, eyes shut, panting listlessly. He was no bigger than a dog, but there was not room for him to stretch out flat.

Athena chirped at Menelik in imitation of his usual kittenish greeting. The lion's ears pricked in acknowledgment and he blinked, but he closed his eyes again and lay quiet.

Oh, Telemakos thought in sudden panic, I want him *out of here.*

Tiny grains of sand were printing themselves into Telemakos's grazed knees like a branding iron, burning hot. He glanced over his shoulder and spotted the ship's master.

"Can I have the lion on its lead, now we're off the ship? Can I take it to the king myself—" Telemakos remembered Abreha's title in South Arabian. "I mean, to the najashi? I want to see the city."

"Yes, all right," said his grandfather's agreeable captain. "Abreha stays in the governor's mansion when he's in al-Muza. Look, you can see it from here. It's the great white house on the rise behind the city. The way is clear if you follow the principal avenues."

Telemakos fought with the cage's sliding bolts. The wood around them had swollen in the humid air, and Telemakos pinched his fingers getting the door open. He spat and swore.

"Damn, damn, damn," repeated his small sister.

"Shhh," Telemakos said, mortified. She would repeat anything. "That was naughty of me. Kiss my poor fingers."

He got the door open, but Menelik would not come out. The lion stayed pressed against the back of the cage, cramped and miserable. Telemakos had to crawl in halfway after him, shuffling bent low, with Athena clinging to his neck like a bag of lead weights.

"Ah, Menelik, Menelik, my bold one, my brave one," Telemakos sang under his breath, fondling the lion behind its ears and kissing its dry nose. "Come now, it's all right, you are the prince of lions—"

Telemakos's head was pressed down by the top of the cage. As he hooked the lead into Menelik's collar, for a single airless second he was imprisoned again, held helpless and blind by hands he could not see. He struggled, and banged his head on the hutch. Dazed, he backed out quickly, still gripping the lion's lead, and Menelik followed. Telemakos sat back on his heels, clinging to Athena and breathing hard, awash with relief to find himself back in al-Muza.

Telemakos looked across the edge of the sand at the city before him. He was weighed down by the baby on his hip and the satchel over his shoulder, and his single hand was going to have to be wholly devoted to controlling the lion. Maybe I should wait for the porters, he thought.

He glanced at the empty cage and slammed it shut with a sharp kick.

"Good-bye, traveling hutch. *Never again.*"

They crossed the mooring beach and set out to discover al-Muza.

X

THE HANGED MAN

THE AIR SMELLED of sweet incense and stinking fish, like unrefined ambergris. All the walls and domes were washed with gypsum plaster, and the city sparkled as though it lay beneath a film of salt. Deire must have been like this, Telemakos thought, our port city lost to plague. White Deire, they used to call it.

The lion cut a path for Telemakos through the suq markets, like Moses parting the Red Sea. Athena kept her head up and alert, staring at purple men beating cloth with indigo, or blind-folded camels turning oil presses. In an alley of saddlers' stalls and shops, Telemakos stopped to examine a row of colored belts and scabbards, considering a new strap for Athena's slip-ping harness. He was kneeling before the vendor's carpet with Menelik's lead held down beneath one foot when he caught the scent of basil, freshly broken. He tensed himself for conflict.

A clutch of curious local children had gathered in his wake. Now they were passing fragrant sprigs of green surreptitiously among themselves, tucking it up one another's sleeves and be-hind their ears. They spoke a local dialect of Ethiopic so mixed with South Arabian that at first Telemakos could make no sense of them at all, but he recognized what they were doing: warding off ill fortune. He stood up and turned to face them. Taking care not to touch his eyes, he shaded his face with his wrist at his hairline and his head bent, so that his terrible dead man's gaze did not fall on anyone. It was the safest way to ap-proach a host of strange children.

Athena copied him, covering her face with both hands. Then she suddenly threw her arms wide and announced, "Baby!" She reached up to pull at her brother's fingers so the others could see his face. "Boy!"

Everybody laughed.

"Aksumite?" a girl asked in comprehensible Greek, the common language of the Red Sea. She wore a blue headscarf sewn with a fringe of jingling pale gold shells across her fore-head. "We thought you were Socotran. There is a township on the island where all the people have blue eyes."

"What a fearful lot of basil the other Socotrans must con-sume," Telemakos said.

One or two of them sheepishly tossed aside their sprigs.

"The king's wife is of that village," continued the shell girl, "and you do look like the king's children." She flicked a finger at Athena's bracelet. "Your baby sister could be Queen Muna's daughter come to life again. The princess was born here, four years ago, her last child; the queen spent her confinement here instead of San'a because she had such a craving for fish. I remember when the najashi came for her, he held up the baby on the terrace of the archon's mansion and said that her name was Amirah. My mother took me to see. They are all dead now, my mother, the king's children, Queen Muna's children, and his first queen Khirash's children, Asad his heir and his favorite; they all died of plague." She twisted her mouth wryly, as if to show how little this meant to anyone. "You know how it is."

Telemakos did not know how it was. He looked down briefly and pressed his own lips together in grim sympathy.

"What are you buying, then, Aksumite?" asked an older boy who towered over the others. "A sword belt?"

"A muzzle," Telemakos answered coolly. He knelt again and picked up Menelik's lead. The children all looked down at Menelik, who had been lying quietly in the shade beneath a screen hung with boot laces and sandal straps.

"That's not a dog," one said, and they edged away.

Telemakos gave them his father's crooked, incomplete smile, and said amiably, "Maybe you can help me. I need a tailor to mend my sister's harness, but I do not know who would best do the work."

"Oh, that's business for the girls—" A boy whose face was cratered with smallpox scars started to walk away, but the big one asked suddenly, "Is the lion tamed? Will it let me touch it?"

Telemakos noted that they were simply a gathered audience, not a real gang; they had no leader.

"You can hold him while the harness is being mended, if you like," Telemakos said. "I'll have enough to do with the baby."

"Not I, thank you!"

The other boys laughed at the tall one. Telemakos let his breath out slowly in a private sigh of relief. They would not mob him now.

They gave Telemakos conflicting directions. The girl with the shell scarf and the big boy argued briefly in their strange dialect, and were told off by the belt salesman for treading on his carpet. "Step back," Telemakos told them, pulling Menelik up close to him, and of the merchant he asked politely, "Which of them speaks truly, sir?"

"Iskinder will lead you aright," said the scabbard seller, pointing to the tall one. "Call him Alexander, if you prefer Greek. His uncle sends me my best customers."

Telemakos looked the children over as he fell in step beside tall Iskinder. They were all reasonably well dressed. The little boys wore wooden daggers, and the older boys wore real ones, in wide, curved, ornate scabbards. The girls carried shopping baskets. Everyone's wrists and ears rang with silver jewelry. Gedar's children would have looked ragged and beggarly among them.

"I'd forgotten the smell of cinnamon till I landed here today," said Telemakos. "All our ports have been closed for the last three years. Your country seems very prosperous to me."

"So it is," said tall Iskinder. "Arabia the Fortunate. But you did not see it in the great sickness, when there were not enough of us to bury our own dead. People dumped corpses in the sea. Everything stank."

"Ships still came in, but the king stayed away," said the girl, shaking her head so that her shells chittered. "The najashi hid in the Hanish Islands for half a year, when plague was here, so he would not die with the rest of his countrymen. All his children died. He thought they would be all right in San'a, in the mountains, but the frankincense merchants brought the sickness there as well."

"He has no heir," said the scarred one. "The najashi would send all the frankincense and salt back where it came from if it could bring his sons to life again."

Telemakos could not tell, from their talk, if they approved of their king or not. When they spoke of their dead it was with a resigned and eerie indifference that was alien to him.

"These suqs used to be much more crowded," said the shell girl. "My grandmother likes it better now. Doing the shopping is like a long day of visiting. The merchants chatter at you till your ears drop off, and give you coffee. It will take you most of the afternoon to agree on a price for your baby carrier."

They led Telemakos by the city's secret ways, along passages so narrow that the ibex horns guarding the rooftops against ill spirit met overhead like the bars of a twisted cage.

"Why are you in Himyar?"

Telemakos brushed close to the white walls on his right so that Athena would not hit the building on the left, and when the sunlight caught them between lanes, he found his shamma glinting with gypsum. Menelik's fur, too, was frosted with it.

"Why are you in Himyar?"

Telemakos, absorbed in mentally mapping the intricate pattern of al-Muza's alleyways, realized suddenly that one of his guides was talking to him.

"Why are you in Himyar?" Iskinder asked for the third time.

"I'm to deliver this lion to the najashi. It's a gift from the emperor of Aksum."

"Are you employed by the emperor?" Iskinder's voice cracked on the final word of each sentence he uttered.

The group emerged all at once into a wide, bright plaza. It was noisy with fountains and traffic and seagulls crying and the mourning warble of pigeons.

"Are you employed by the emperor?"

The square was lined with ceremonial thrones like those on the road leading into the imperial city of Aksum, each carved of Aksumite basalt, black against the white lime and white sand of al-Muza's walls and streets.

"Are you employed by the emperor?" Iskinder repeated patiently.

"Only to deliver the lion," Telemakos said. "They sent me because I raised it. It was an honor to be sent, but not an obligation."

There was a faint, ugly smell about the place that reminded Telemakos of the bloody days immediately following his accident.

"You're lucky," Iskinder said. "It's good to have connections. I mean to join the city guard here in another year or so, but I have no one to recommend me, so there is no reason they should take me in."

"Of course they will take you in," said one of the other boys. "You are a giant. So what if you're afraid of that lion?"

"I did not see you volunteer to hold it," Iskinder retorted. Telemakos pulled Menelik against his thigh and brushed glitter from the lion's cheeks and whiskers.

"Poor feet," Athena remarked.

"What did you say, Tena?"

The girl with the shells suddenly spoke quietly in Telemakos's ear. "You might like to cover your sister's eyes. There was an execution yesterday, and it may frighten her."

She turned aside and pointed skyward.

"*Mother of God,*" Telemakos swore in a whisper, and Menelik pressed even tighter against his leg as Telemakos jerked up the lion's lead so he could pull the end of his shamma over Athena's head.

Not three paces away from them, but above them, was the man who was to have been killed the day before. He was still alive. His execution had been carried out, indeed, but he was still alive. He had been crucified, nailed to a length of mast wood and left to die, and he hung above the street like a parody of the young Christian god, struggling and gasping in the scorching meridian sun, hours after he should have died of thirst or shock.

Athena was trying to untangle her face.

"Do not look, Tena," Telemakos rasped. He stood directly beneath the bare, blood-streaked feet, so close that were he taller he could have reached up and brushed away the flies that clustered busily over the blackening wounds.

Athena twisted herself free.

"You hide again," Telemakos whispered.

Athena fought with her brother, refusing to make a game of it. "Feet," she said. "Poor feet."

Telemakos took a deep breath, struggling for control of his stomach. He remembered to keep hold of the lion. *Walk away! One step, another, in a dozen paces it will be gone.*

He mastered himself. He could not walk away, passionlessly, pretending he had seen nothing. He stood still, looked up, and said clearly to the dying man, "Peace to you. God rest you."

The children around him broke into a babel of astonishment and censure.

"The najashi ought to whip you!"

"Bless him? Are you mad? He is a condemned traitor!"

"You don't talk to a *dead man!*"

Telemakos turned on the pack that had driven him here, and said in quick, accusatory fury, "Does it matter whether or not anyone talks to him? However evil he may be, he is suffering for it now, and I wish him rest."

They were silent around him for a moment, eyes wide with disbelief or narrowed in disapproving frowns, appalled by such daring.

Then Iskinder, who perhaps needed to prove his own daring again after his refusal to hold the lion, shouted a word up to the miserable creature lingering above them.

"Scorpion!"

Dread lit in Telemakos like wildfire.

Once, hunting in the Aksumite highlands, Telemakos and his father had been caught on an open hillside during a dry storm so intense that the charged sky had pulled Medraut's fine hair out around his head in a silver halo and made the down on Telemakos's arms and legs prick as though he were being stung by sand driven in a gale. The foreboding that wrapped Telemakos now was as compelling as the force of that silent lightning.

"Ho, Scorpion!"

Astonishingly, horribly, the transfixed man opened his eyes.

"Here is one of your fellow countrymen who wants to bless you, you treacherous, double-dealing cur," Iskinder called up.

The man's hot eyes turned on Telemakos, and they looked at each other for too long a moment.

Then, as if by some terrible enchantment, the condemned one came vividly alive and found the strength to pour forth in a croaking hiss: "The mute has found his tongue at last! You are a long way from the salt mines in Afar, silent little sneak, and you did not wear such fine clothes then, when you sold your freedom for a mouthful of water. All those weeks before they came for you I thought you must be one of Gebre Meskal's jackals, I swore to it, I knew in my bones you were blinding me to something—*Who sent you?*"

It was Hara. It was Hara, the corrupt foreman from the salt mines, faceless Hara of the scorpion's pincers—Telemakos glanced unwisely at the impaled hands, to assure himself they were really hands, and saw there a living horror worse than any of his dreams.

"Who sent you? What bitter god sends you to me now, to taunt me that I did not cut out your tongue when I was advised to? *Why should I want or need your jackal's blessing on my dying breath?*" Hara spat venomously, scarcely human anymore, a living cadaver. "A curse on such a blessing. Let the najashi hang you up in my place next, you unholy creeping mongrel spy! A curse on your blessing! *A curse on the lot of you*—"

This went beyond anyone's endurance. The children scattered, muttering charms and prayers, touching the leaves of basil and crossing themselves and covering their eyes. Telemakos had a fleeting impression of their hands fluttering like a flock of doves taking suddenly to wing.

"An evil dream," Hara sighed. "Yes, it is only a dream," he told himself, and closed his eyes.

Telemakos, too, closed his eyes, as the white square whirled red and black around him. He fought off the nausea but lost his footing and crashed heavily onto one knee.

"Come away," said a low voice in his ear.

Iskinder had not deserted him. Iskinder had firm hold of Menelik's lead, and pulled Telemakos to his feet. Athena was shrieking. Telemakos's fall had frightened her into tears, and he had not even noticed.

"For God's sake, come away. I am very sorry I said anything—"

"I too!" Telemakos gasped.

"Come on—"

Athena continued to scream. The lion growled low in its throat. Iskinder led them beyond Hara's hearing and his fading sight; they crossed the square to sit on the far edge of one of the fountains. Gulls scattered and settled again on the black thrones as they passed.

"Here, take your lion back, I'll draw you a drink."

Telemakos twined the leash around his ankle and bent to his howling sister. "It's all right, little owlet, hush now." He reached into the spray and dripped water over Athena's sweaty hands. Menelik nosed between them, licking at the baby's fingers. "Stop that, your tongue's too rough." Telemakos pushed the fond, heavy head away. The big boy came back with a dipper of water.

"Thank you." Telemakos tried to drink, but he could not hold the dipper steady. Iskinder took it back and waited patiently for the shuddering to quiet.

"That wretch thought he knew you," Iskinder said.

"I have never seen him before in my life," Telemakos vowed, and it was true. Hara had kept him blindfolded for longer than two months. Telemakos would never have known him if Hara had not recognized him first.

"They say crazy things, sometimes, while they're hanging there. Come now, baby, stop your hullabaloo. Can you drink from a cup? Show your brother how to do it." Iskinder held the dipper to Athena's lips. It was nearly as big as her head. She took hold of it with both hands and drank as though she were dying of thirst.

The sharp, cool part of Telemakos's mind that could stand at a distance from the rest of him observed, This boy is behaving nobly.

"Your friends will all wave their sprigs of basil at you now, and run away from you, for being mad enough to stick with my fell company," Telemakos said.

"Oh, well," the boy answered without rancor, still holding the dipper up for Athena. "He cursed the guard, too, when they brought him here yesterday. It is three months since he was condemned; I think he must have spent all that time thinking up the ugliest way to damn his executioners. If I'm to join their ranks, I may as well get used to it."

Telemakos frowned, staring over his shoulder through the fountain and squinting, trying to pull some sense out of the shock.

"Who is he? What had he done?"

"He'd been smuggling. He was a pirate," Iskinder said. Athena pushed the dipper away and turned back to Telemakos to wipe her face on his shamma. "They announced it at the execution. He ran the customs office here for the past two years, cheating the city. But he was arrested because he'd financed a plot against the king. So he was probably a spy as well, or some other agent of a rival nation. Perhaps Aksum, his own nation. They wouldn't announce that. They wouldn't risk offending the Aksumite emperor. But all the talk is that he was a spy. It's often a spy's death."

Telemakos again scooped water from the fountain and dashed it over his head. Athena clung to him like a barnacle, scrubbing her hot face against his shoulder.

Now I know, he thought. Now I know what happened to Hara.

"I would never make a city guard," Telemakos said in a low voice. "I would never have the stomach for it. I think I would rather take such punishment myself than have to deal it out."

He splashed more water down his neck. It was tepid, sweltering as the air.

"Your courage must stretch a long way further than mine, then," said the young man named for Alexander. "I could not even speak such a thought aloud, bare minutes after being cursed to such a fate."

It was close to sundown when Telemakos climbed the broad public stairway to the archon's mansion. He felt crushed by the length and breadth of that day: the stifling heat; the strange city; the edgy, urban children; the hours spent carrying Athena while keeping the lion on leash. And so back to Hara. What did it feel like, what did you think, when they were driving the nails in? It had not been a dream. It was real.

There was a party of Hadrami legates standing on the archon's terrace discussing the impending annual Great Assembly of the Himyar Federation. They were hard, turbaned men representing the warrior tribes of the wadi valley that bordered the northeastern Arabian desert; they wore robes of sweeping iridescent indigo and great, curved daggers, and they were greeting and saluting the al-Muza officials while their salukis waited free but obedient at their heels.

Telemakos pushed Menelik gently to the ground and knelt there with the lion to admire the dogs and wait for them to leave. The sun was smoldering lower over the Red Sea through the sullen haze at his back.

"Look at the dogs, my owlet," Telemakos whispered in his sister's ear. She had not napped that day, and he knew her mood was as brittle as his.

"Boy's hair?" she requested, twisting and pulling at it.

"Shhh."

The dogs were breathtaking. They were lean and sleek, with long, silken fur; Menelik, who was no taller than they, seemed heavy and awkward by comparison. The gazelle hounds twitched their long noses in the lion's direction, gazing with interest at this strange creature: foe or prey or ally? Bound by courtly obedience but tense with curiosity, they moved only their noses. They reminded Telemakos of himself.

At Telemakos's other side, Menelik made silly chirping

noises. Grandfather's hounds had tolerated him indulgently, and he was used to dogs. Telemakos began to ache with the strain of holding him in check.

"Hush—lie quiet—when they've gone, we'll find the naja-shi—"

Menelik barked.

In seconds Telemakos became the center of everyone's attention, surrounded by a swirl of blue robes and gilded dagger hilts and the long, curious, soulful faces of the salukis. "Good dogs," Telemakos said under his breath, to reassure Athena rather than calm the dogs. But she was anything but frightened. She started panting in imitation of them and grabbed for their silken ears and long noses. Telemakos tried to hold her hands back, and suddenly, without warning, Menelik's lead slipped through his fingers.

The lion moved free of Telemakos, slow and proud and without fear, until it stood calm and at ease in a circle of salukis. Menelik let them sniff him all over and butted noses with them. The men broke into a chorus of astonishment, and some delight, in formal South Arabian.

"What folly's this?"

"Well trained, your Dancer."

"No fear."

"Back, Windcutter, back, Redbelly, my fine girl—"

"Watch that thing's teeth!"

What a fuss, Telemakos thought.

"They're only milk teeth," he said stiffly, loud enough to be heard well over men and dogs. "The lion's not six months old. He can't tear meat yet."

He did not expect the clear treble of his voice to ring with such damning scorn.

The men fell silent and stared at Telemakos. Then one of the chieftains bowed to him with exaggerated courtesy.

"He is hiding his crown in his pocket," the man explained to his companions, and they fell about laughing. Then they cut Telemakos low with ridicule.

"His queen sits in his other pocket."

"He travels with all his court about him."

"How many paces does it take to measure your dominion, little sheik?"

Telemakos bent his head before them, his cheeks burning, knowing he deserved this. What a day. He glanced upward through his lashes for an instant and saw that Abreha Anbessa, the Lion Hunter of Himyar, najashi over all the Arabs of the coastal plains and the highlands, stood in their midst.

The najashi wore a linen head cloth like any Aksumite noble, bound about his temples by a narrow rope of coiled gold. His skin was considerably darker than that of the Himyar natives, and Telemakos was reminded that he and the najashi were countrymen, though he would have recognized him anyway by the heavy brow that made him so like his brother Priamos. Abreha had sensibly and firmly taken hold of Menelik's lead.

"Dogs, dogs, dogs!" Athena told them all.

"Pardon, pardon, gentle masters," Telemakos apologized

with due humility. "I am ashamed. I am your servant."

Abreha cut him off with his own name, speaking with fond recognition and no surprise.

"Lij Telemakos Meder, at last. My sheiks, my brothers, cry welcome to this prince, and do not mock him. I expect he does not yet have the measure of his dominion."

Abreha pushed aside one of the dogs. He knelt with one arm lying fearlessly along the lion's back and looked Telemakos up and down in silence.

"You are not the same child I met seven years ago," the najashi said at last. "Did I not warn you to beware Solomon's teeth? Do you remember?"

"I shall surely take better heed of your warnings in future," Telemakos said.

"Your tongue is still as silver as your hair, Lij Telemakos." Abreha's attendants chuckled in agreement. "Or Beloved Telemakos, as Gebre Meskal names you in his letter. How you are favored! That was my father's title, too. Well, I could ask no better fortune than that the son of Medraut of Britain grace my court this year. Where have you been all afternoon, you elusive young jackal? Your recommendations came straight to me, instead of dawdling about the city with their wayward owner."

"I did not think! Again pardon—" Telemakos bit down on his silver tongue to keep it still, and lifted the najashi's free hand to his lips to kiss it ceremonially. Abreha wore a heavy intaglio ring of some dull metal, pewter-sheened as a storm cloud. It was engraved with his mark, the lion's head within the five-rayed star.

The great ring was level with Athena's chin. Copying Telemakos, she seized the najashi's dark, narrow hand in both of hers and kissed the impression of the lion. Her bracelet from Gedar jangled. She gazed at the king of Himyar with her luminous eyes, her nose still pressed against his ring.

"Lion," she said.

His courtiers burst into laughter. She was talking about the picture on his ring, but it sounded as though she were addressing him.

Abreha let the baby linger over the glowering sigil.

"It is supposed to have belonged to Solomon," he told Telemakos, "passed down all the ages from father to son. It is the crest of my father, Ras Bitwoded Anbessa, the Lion of Wedem. Asad, my eldest son, who is dead now, was named 'lion' like my father, but in South Arabian."

Still he did not take his hand away. "She's wise for her years, this bright-eyed enchantress you carry with you. Athena, is it? The goddess of wisdom! Most appropriate." The najashi smiled. His full smile was a surprise, breaking his unhappy frown with joy and light. "Young Princess, Emebet Athena Meder. You are welcome to my kingdom."

Telemakos did not think he had ever heard anyone call his sister by her title and full name. He looked down at her as if seeing a different girl there: a small royal lady who could charm a king with a word and a kiss, with hair like a cloud of spun bronze and eyes of gray crystal.

And what do I look like, he wondered as an afterthought. What do they see first: my white hair, my one arm, my sorcerous eyes?

Abreha showed no sign that he noticed any of these things.

"Look at this, my sheiks, my brothers," the king of Himyar announced. "We have lost Himyar's rising generation, but we are gifted now with Britain's."

"Goewin Dragon's Daughter would never send you such treasures, my najashi, if she knew what a wolf you are," said one of the turbaned men.

"She knows what I am," Abreha answered softly.

Athena still had hold of the najashi's hand. He raised the children both at once, drawing on Athena to bring Telemakos to his feet. "You need not kneel to these men, Lij Telemakos," said the najashi. "All princes are of equal merit in my Federation. I guide them, but I do not rule them. *Najashi* is the South Arabian word for 'king,' but my formal title is a more ancient word, *mukarrib*, 'federator.'"

He stood with Telemakos at his side and ruffled the short scruff at the back of Menelik's neck. He said to his companions, "We'll let the young lion learn to run with the salukis, eh?"

XI

STAIRWAYS

TELEMAKOS SPENT MOST of the next day sitting in the shade of the colonnaded courtyard and composing a letter to his mother. The first part was easy, telling of his journey and Athena's adventures on the ship. He drew a sketch of Athena sitting in a boat, smiling and waving her wooden giraffe, which he hoped would make his mother laugh. He assured Turunesh that Abreha Anbessa was happy to accept both children into his household.

It was more difficult to word the cryptic information Telemakos wanted to embed in this bland report. He practiced his message to Goewin in wax and let Athena rub it out with her fist, until he had what he wanted to say by heart and could transcribe it directly onto a palm strip without leaving any legible trace of his false starts:

Please send my love also to my father and my aunt. My father should be thankful I am here with the lion, for I have seen it kill a scorpion. I am glad it is bold but I hope it does not happen again.

Telemakos had no doubt that Goewin would decipher this the first time she heard it. The meaning seemed so plain to him he had misgivings about letting it go, but no one questioned that he should let his mother know he had arrived safely. No one even asked to look at the letter, let alone censor it. Abreha sealed it with his own mark, to speed its passage.

Two days later they started for San'a. The najashi traveled modestly, on foot, with an entourage of half a dozen men and three camels, and Telemakos carried Athena. She was a good traveler. Medraut had sewn several pockets into the side of her harness, and she would spend most of a march fitting a stalk of sugar cane into each of these by turns before she finally decided to teethe on it. She switched at flies with an ostrich feather, for Telemakos as well as herself.

"How many weeks has it been since either one of you used a comb, boy?" Abreha asked him. It was after sundown; the worst of the low-lying Hot Lands were behind them, and they were about to enter the wadi valley that channeled the mountain rainwater. They had found grazing for the camels and set snares for sandgrouse to feed the lion. Now they sat in firelight over the evening meal. "You'll soon find things nesting in your hair."

"We're both perfectly nit free just now," Telemakos answered defensively.

"I mean mice, or birds."

Telemakos laughed.

"Give me your comb, Boulos," the najashi said to one of his companions. The soldiers wore their long hair plaited and buttered sleekly against their scalps. "Now, will the young princess Emebet Athena let me untangle her bright hair? Come here, my honey badger."

Telemakos had never seen her so indulgent of a stranger. She steadied herself against the najashi and pulled at his bushy eyebrows and chewed on the signet ring that was said to have belonged to King Solomon. Then she sat contentedly in Abreha's lap and let him pick through her hair for a full ten minutes or so before demanding, "Tena do."

Her arms were still so babily disproportionate to her body that she could scarcely reach the top of her own head. If she did manage it, she would not draw the teeth through her hair, in case she pulled it.

"Boy," she said, and waved the comb at Telemakos. "Boy's hair. Tena do."

He bent his head to her, to let her try. She was gentler than his mother. She trawled through the tips of Telemakos's hair with the mesmerizing, absorbed patience of a cat washing itself.

I'll let her do it every day, he thought. In a year or two she'll do it properly, and I won't have to ask for help.

"They share everything," Boulos observed. "Did you see them this afternoon, brother and sister, taking turns drinking from the same goatskin bottle?"

"Aye," said Abreha thoughtfully. "They hold it between them."

Telemakos said, "We shoot together, too. She holds the stones, I the sling."

The soldiers clapped and laughed, enchanted. "Seeing is believing! Show us, show us!"

Abreha stopped Telemakos from reaching for his sling.

"We are not a traveling circus," the najashi said in a low firm voice, reminding Telemakos again of his own father.

Athena crawled away from Telemakos in the night to cuddle up with the lion. Left alone on the warm, dry ground at the edge of the Himyarite Hot Lands, Telemakos dreamed he was sharing a meal of injera bread and fasting food, no meat, with a man who had a lion's head and a scorpion's hands. They were feeding each other, by way of honor. The lion's teeth snatched the thin bread and greens from Telemakos's finger-tips with fearful enthusiasm. He will eat me next, Telemakos kept thinking, there is not enough here to satisfy him.

Abreha's hand on his forehead woke him to snarling battle.

"Get away from my eyes!"

It was early morning. The scrubland where they were camped was veiled in blue light; the sun was not yet up.

"Mercy on us, child," said Abreha softly. "What is wrong with your eyes?"

The other men were awake, busy with the camels and the

cooking fire. Menelik was sitting upright, tethered to his stake, calmly washing himself. Athena slept on, pressed against the lion's thigh with her arms and legs tucked beneath her.

"I—" Telemakos did not know how to answer. *Never lie to Abreha,* his mother had warned him. "I was dreaming. I—" He could not tell Abreha of the salt mines. "When my eyes are covered, I—" He hesitated. "I have ugly dreams, sometimes, since my accident. It was through protecting my head that I lost my arm."

It was not untrue, just indirect.

"I know how it is with nightmares," Abreha said, and blinked agreement, understanding. "But you were wide awake the instant I touched you. You will have to learn to control that."

It dawned on Telemakos that he must seem shockingly undisciplined. He made a formal apology, on his knees, with his forehead against the dry ground.

"Forgive me, my najashi. I dishonor you, forgetting myself over a dream."

"Get off your knees," Abreha said mildly. "I thought you might like to come check the snares with me. Leave the baby; Boulos will see she comes to no harm."

Abreha waited for Telemakos to twist on his shamma, and they set out along one of the antelope trails through the scrubby acacia.

"I like traveling simply," Abreha said. "I like to hunt and

set snares for my own meat, and watch it cook on a fire I have built myself." There was a rock partridge in the first snare, and Abreha knelt to undo it. "I would not want to be helpless in the hands of my servants."

Telemakos watched. Abreha worked with his left hand resting casually on his hip, his thumb hooked in his knife belt. He unpicked the snare with his right hand only, moving with effortless efficiency, and knotted the wires around the bird's red legs with his teeth. It was impossible to know whether he was doing it with only one hand on purpose, to make a point, or if he always hunted this way.

He gave the partridge to Telemakos to carry. "We will stop your dreams somehow," he said. "Or keep them from troubling you when you are awake, at any rate. I will think about it."

Then he stood up and strode whistling mournfully toward the next snare.

He is *kinder* than my father, Telemakos thought. I am glad to be here.

In three weeks they came to San'a's walled towers, glittering a full mile and a half above the sea, in a plain of rich grain fields and orchards of apricot and almond. "This gate leads to the Street of Shade," Abreha told Telemakos as they entered the city. The tall houses rose around them in blocks of light and shadow, paint and whitewash. "Look! All the road ahead lies in the shadow of Maharib Ghumdan, the tiered palaces, Himyar's heart. People think Ghumdan was built by Solomon."

They passed into the palace. The lower stories were dark and cool, musty with horse and goat. Endless marble stairways made a backbone to the great building; the corridors were lit by narrow windows with intricate alabaster frames and small, jewel-colored windowpanes. The pale stone walls caught the colored light in pools and crevices. On the fourth level they met a tall, older man with a handsome mustache, who strode forward to greet the najashi.

"You are unexpected, your majesty! Welcome! My God, what is that? A lion? How old is it?" His clothes were the same deep blue as the Hadramis' robes, and he wore a sword as well as a dagger.

"Tharan." Abreha returned his greeting. They held each other by the forearms and rubbed noses with each other. "I am glad to see you, my lieutenant." Telemakos waited, listening, as they spoke over his head. "What news is there?"

"Your British ambassador has gone, dismissed one week ago. You did not pass him on the road, then?"

Abreha raised his eyebrows, as the local children and Abreha's soldiers did to say that something was not so. "Not that we knew. Well, Godspeed to Gwalchmei of Britain. We have Artos's grandson here now. Do you remember Lij Telemakos Meder, of the house of Nebir, who caught Gebre Meskal's lions?" Abreha handed over Menelik's lead to his lieutenant. "Telemakos is here to study under his uncle, Dawit Star Master. And this is his sister."

Telemakos wanted very much to know what the British

ambassador had done to warrant his dismissal, but it would be boldly impudent to interrupt the introductions with such a question.

"Your lady Queen Muna will delight to have a baby in the nursery again," Tharan said.

"I'll take Telemakos to meet the children, and join you in my study presently," Abreha told him.

They left the lion with Tharan and climbed higher. Telemakos counted eight stories and still they were not at the top. It reminded Telemakos of the journey up the staired ways of the wadi valley they had climbed to get into the al-Surat Mountains; they had had to trade the baggage camels for mules to make their way up wide basalt flights set between terraces of hanging grapes and frankincense. Telemakos had carried Athena most of the way. It felt as though he had done nothing but climb stairs for the last ten days.

"I had hoped to meet Gwalchmei," Telemakos said. "He is my father's cousin. They were raised as foster brothers."

"It's poor luck you've missed each other," Abreha agreed. "Had you arrived a fortnight earlier you would have met, or had he known you were coming, he might have stayed. But he has just heard that his father is dead—King Lot of the Orcades is dead. Gwalchmei's duty lies in Britain now, so I have dismissed him."

"Oh."

Goewin had not told Telemakos about this. Or maybe she had not heard it yet.

They continued up the stairs. It all seemed strangely quiet. They passed courtiers and servants, but not nearly enough to make Ghumdan seem busy, the bustling heart of a flourishing kingdom. Abreha's palace was full of holes. It was rich and beautiful and empty.

At last they came into a great hall near the top. The room was garlanded with dried rose and cinnamon, and lemon and mint leaves, knit together in imitation of vines heavy with fruit. The windows were set with carnelian and citrine, and the white ceiling was veiled in a painted trellis of green leaves. Hanging from the ceiling was a score of silver birdhouses filled with songbirds. And though Telemakos had never seen anything like this in his life, it seemed so familiar it made his skin crawl.

What does this remind me of? It was something Goewin told me once . . . Something in Homer? A story, a British legend? Yes, I heard it from Goewin. What did she say? We woke to find the Queen's Garden a riot of caged songbirds. . . .

He had it then. His grandmother kept songbirds, his British grandmother, Morgause, who had crippled Medraut's hand to punish him, and had once offered Goewin's weight in silver for proof of her death. And the story was that his grandmother had hung a hundred songbirds in cages in a garden and lured Lleu, the young prince of Britain, there and then tore open his wrist with her nails and tried to poison him.

"Bird," said Athena in astonishment. "Bird!" The birds chattered and fluted, and she answered three different calls in perfect imitation of each song. "Bird!" she cried, reaching toward the silver cages.

Telemakos took a few hesitant steps forward, to bring her closer.

"This is the children's room," said Abreha. "Hello there, Malika. Have you missed me?"

Telemakos lowered his gaze. There were half a dozen children sitting in a circle on the cushions by the low windows, watching critically as one of the bigger girls dipped indigo out of a soapstone pot and constructed a crude tracery of palm leaves over another girl's face.

"Najashi!"

They clamored around Abreha. He sat with them before the windows, the girl with the painted face on his lap. He beckoned to Telemakos to sit as well, and the children bunched together to make room for him. They reminded him of roosting hens.

Telemakos sat down and unbuckled Athena. She climbed free of her harness and began to roll and tumble in the cushions with joyful abandon. The children stared at Telemakos for a moment, noticing his imperfection, then quickly looked away.

"Where are the others, Malika?" Abreha asked.

The girl with the painted face answered. She was proud and self-possessed, and Telemakos had the impression she queened it over the rest of them. "The Star Master wanted some lapis lazuli for his new globe, and the Lady Muna has gone with him

to the jewelers' suq. They have taken Lu'lu. The rest of them
are watching the guards' parade."

"I have brought you a new brother and sister. This is Lij
Telemakos Meder of the house of Nebir, and the little princess
Emebet Athena. Their grandfather is a vizier in the Aksumite
imperial court. Their other grandfather was high king of
Britain."

Telemakos bowed his head to Abreha's adopted children.
They nodded politely in return.

Abreha patted Athena's stomach. She was lying on her
back in the cushions, pointing up at the ceiling and counting
to herself rapturously, as though she had suddenly found herself
in paradise. "Bird. Bird and bird. Bird bird."

"Athena will stay in the nursery, and with you here in the
children's room during the day. Telemakos is the Star Master's
student, and he is to sleep in the Great Globe Room, off the
scriptorium. Show him, Malika. Show him our home. I will
have supper with you, but I have promised to hear Tharan's
report first. Telemakos, Athena, my young family will make you
welcome now. This artist with the face paints is Inas; this very
pretty one is Malika. It will take you a little time to learn all
their names. There are fourteen of them altogether, my Royal
Scions. They are princes and princesses every one, heirs to
Himyar's tribal kingdoms."

The najashi left, after a deal of rubbing of noses and
pressing of hands, and once more Telemakos found himself
at the mercy of a clutch of strange children. Directly follow-

ing Abreha's departure, Malika, the girl with the painted face, told him, "I shall be queen of Sheba when a husband is found for me."

"Shall you?" Telemakos repeated in some disbelief.

"It is the old kingdom of Sheba," Malika said loftily. "It used to be bigger, but it is still Sheba." She looked him up and down and asked the question they were clearly all dying to ask: "What happened to you?"

"I had a fight with a lion."

They gasped in awe and admiration. Two of them began to whisper frantically together.

"Lion or lioness?" asked a dark, thin boy with his hair done up the way Abreha's soldiers had worn theirs. "Was it fully grown?"

Telemakos felt like an imposter, then, because there had been nothing heroic about his accident. It was not an honorable wound, got in battle or in the hunt; it was a glaring memorial to his greatest ever moment of stupidity.

"One of the emperor's pets did it, in Aksum," he said. "I was careless. I was ill for a long time after, half the year and more."

"Is that what turned your hair white?"

Telemakos laughed. Maybe he could blame all his peculiarities on this one incident. "I was born with that. My father has hair like mine. His skin is white, too."

"He must look like a ghoul."

"He can be very frightening," Telemakos agreed.

"He must look like Gwalchmei of Britain," Inas, the big girl who was doing the face painting, said sensibly. "His hair was red, but his beard was as fair as your hair."

"They were foster brothers. They're cousins. Gwalchmei is my kinsman. I've never met him, though."

One of the little girls patted Athena on the stomach, as Abreha had done. Athena sat up quickly, eyed the girl with deep suspicion, and crawled into Telemakos's lap.

"What of your eyes?" said Malika. "And the baby's? Your eyes are like Queen Muna's. You have the eyes of a Socotran."

Oh, Telemakos thought, not this again.

"We are Socotran," he said rebelliously. "Dawit Alta'ir the Star Master is our uncle. Our great-grandmother was his elder sister."

"You are related to everybody!" said the big girl, Inas. "That makes you some-cousin kin to the najashi. The Star Master is Queen Muna's father." She paused only for a moment, as though to take a breath, and then produced a calculation so rapid it was astonishing: "You would be second cousins once removed to the najashi's children, if they had lived. Small wonder he is anxious to welcome you. He has no nearer lineage. He will treat you as his own son and daughter."

"As he does all the Scions!" said Malika, the queen of Sheba. "Do you hear that, little baby girl? You are our sister. Shall you play with us while Telemakos goes to see the Globe Room? Take him aloft, Shadi. The Star Master likes you."

"All right, come on," the dark boy said agreeably, and stood up.

Telemakos hesitated. Athena stood in his lap now, with her arms around his neck, resting her head on his shoulder in a way that declared ownership.

"Come, baby," Inas said. "Stay here with the birds while your brother goes to see his new bed. Look, we can paint you, too." She daubed a swirl of blue across the back of Athena's hand.

Athena screamed. She stared at her hand and shrieked again, and shook her arm furiously as though she could shake the paint off, screeching like fury.

"Sorry—sorry—" Inas was not stupid. She swiped quickly at the indigo streak with a thick towel. "It doesn't hurt, don't cry—"

Telemakos was smothered by Athena's clinging grip. Her carrying on was so disabling that he actually let the other children peel her away from him.

"You do it, baby," Inas said. "You do it to me."

"Look, Tena." Telemakos tried, dipping up fingersful of blue dye. He looked at Inas with one eyebrow raised. "All right, my lady?"

She rolled her eyes and laughed. "Go on, then."

"See, Tena, do it like this." He slashed Inas's face with paint.

"Thanks for that, you pestilent spawn of a desert jackal," she said amiably. "All right, baby, your turn."

Athena stuck one finger tentatively into the makeup pot.

Telemakos slipped away with the boy Shadi. He heard

Athena's screams erupt behind him the second he set foot in the corridor. He looked back over his shoulder, and Shadi started up the stairwell. "Are you coming?"

The sound of Athena's voice never stopped. It faded, but it did not stop. They reached the final story of the Ghumdan palaces and came into Abreha's document room, and the baby's wails continued to reach them, muffled, from the windows on the level below.

The reading room was roofed with a vaulted skylight of alabaster panes so thin you could see the shadows of doves perching on the other side. The translucent stone cast warm yellow light over a circle of low easels, where a gray-haired, senatorial person sat poring over an inventory.

Shadi bowed and excused himself in a whisper to the custodian at the scriptorium's portal, then tiptoed past the scholar. Telemakos followed. His guide pushed open the door to an antechamber, climbed down three steep steps, and beckoned to Telemakos.

"This is the Great Globe Room," Shadi said. "That's the Great Globe. You see."

Telemakos went through the door, down one step, and was so lost in wonder that he could not speak.

The room was filled with stars. The smallest was no bigger than Athena's thumbnail, the largest the size of her fist, and each was crafted of a single quartz crystal set in silver wire. They hung by black cotton thread against a domed ceiling painted black, and seemed to float suspended as effortlessly as real stars. Telemakos was swimming in them until he came down the steps, and then the lowest of them missed the top of his head by an inch. Unthinkingly he reached up, to be among them, and brushed stars aside as he walked into the middle of the room.

Pendent above the highest stars was a globe big enough that Telemakos could have curled inside it. It was figured of leaded glass, and this was painted over in a blue so deep it was nearly black. Its surface was peppered with hundreds of tiny flaws where points had been scratched in the paint.

"A star globe," Telemakos breathed. "Have you seen it alight?"

"The Star Master never lights it anymore. He's going blind. That's why the Lady Muna chooses his equipment for him in the suqs. I expect you'll do it now. Do you know how to read the globe?"

"It would show the positions of the stars against the sky," Telemakos explained, but even as he spoke he realized it was more complex an instrument than that. Lit from within, the globe would cast pinpoint images of the stars against the black dome of the ceiling. And then you could spin the globe to make the stars trace their paths around the heavens.

As Telemakos stood with his eyes fixed above him, the room was suddenly filled with Athena's angry, gasping shouts. He turned around sharply, expecting to see someone standing in the door with her. But there was no one, and Telemakos leaped up the steps and into the upper reading room.

It was quiet there. The man with the inventory did not look up. The noise was coming from the Great Globe Room.

"Come see," Shadi said, kneeling in a corner by the far wall. "This is how Muna and her father talk to each other, so they don't have to go up and down all the stairs."

He was pointing to a hole in the floor. The globe was mounted on a pulley, and this hung down through a shaft leading to the room below. That was where the screams were coming from. "Muna is home," Shadi reported. "She's taken your sister into the nursery. Can you see?"

Telemakos joined him on the floor and looked through the hole. They could see pink light filtering in through the rose-colored windows below, and they could hear the baby in the throes of her tantrum, but they could not see anyone.

"I must go down," Telemakos said.

"Muna will manage her, I promise you, and her sister-slave Rasha endures no nonsense from any child. If Muna's back from market, the Star Master will be up here soon, and he will want to meet you."

Telemakos lay flat on his stomach, with his head hanging halfway between the palace floors. If I call out, he thought, it will upset Athena even more because she won't be able to reach me.

Then she stopped shrieking. The sobs continued, sporadically, as if the baby were still feeling sorry for herself, but something had distracted her enough to calm her down. When her gasping became less frequent, Telemakos could hear a woman's deep, beautiful voice humming a mesmerizing rhythm on four notes, over and over.

"Away. Go away," Athena said viciously.

Shadi tapped him on the shoulder. Telemakos sat up and looked behind him.

"Don't tell me who you are," said the man who stood on the lowest step. "I know your name."

XII

STAR MASTER
AND MORNINGSTAR

HE WAS BAREFOOT. His beard was flyaway and mostly white; around his mouth it was stained an improbable pink. There were leaves—small, glossy leaves—caught in it here and there. His white hair was bound back from his face in a great unruly mare's tail, and Telemakos, who was finding his own hair increasingly difficult to govern, had a sudden mad vision of himself in fifty years.

Shadi held obediently silent. The old man put up his right hand and touched the star that hung nearest it.

"Antares," he said. "The Scorpion's heart."

Telemakos flinched. He said, with childish desperation, "That's not my name."

"Of course not. It's the star's name."

The swinging stars were oriented as though when you entered the room you stood facing northward, at the year's first solstice. That was the Scorpion, hung about the door.

Telemakos looked up; he sat beneath the Phoenix.

The old man came down the last step and reached with his left hand for another star. "Sabik." He let go of Antares, and moved forward his right hand, and his right foot. "Ras Alhague. Head of the man who holds the Serpent."

He was blind, or close to it; his eyes were so milky with cataracts that you could not tell what color they had been. He guided himself across the room by feeling his way from star to star. He stepped toward Telemakos, left hand and left foot.

Telemakos, on both knees, swiftly bent his forehead to the floor in formal reverence.

"Stand up, or I can't see you. I despise ceremony. Gebre Meskal sends me a student, does he? Are you any good? What star is in my hand?"

It took Telemakos a moment to place it correctly, but then he realized its significance. "The flying eagle," Telemakos answered. "Alta'ir."

"Good. You know my name, Dawit Alta'ir, and we need no introduction. By Epiphany you must be able to name all the stars in this room. Can you guess why I have hung the ceiling with stone stars?"

"So you can touch them?"

"It is actually so that I can see them. When the sun shines in the eastern windows, it sets the crystals alight. I have not seen a real star since the great comet of ten years ago. But do not imagine you may hide from me, son of Medraut son of Artos; I shall have no trouble keeping track of you. Detail and color

I give up on, but your silver head is like a great glowing moon among my stars, a bright planet coming and going. Athtar the Morningstar, the forgotten god of South Arabia! Telemakos the Morningstar, prince of the rising generation! Let's start. You may go, Shadi. Shadi, do you know how I know you?"

"I do not, Magus," the thin boy muttered.

"No other king obeys me when I tell him not to speak."

"Thank you, Magus." Shadi excused himself and scuttled away through the door to the scriptorium.

Telemakos watched him go. He wondered how many other of Abreha's orphaned wards had already inherited titles to kingdoms kept in care for them hundreds of miles away.

Dawit Alta'ir sat down on the floor cross-legged next to Telemakos. The leaves in his beard were kat, a mild stimulant of the highlands. They smelled bitter and fresh. Dawit's breath smelled of kat as well, and faintly of rosewater. At his side, against the wall where it would catch light from the eastern windows, there was a low, wide cabinet. Mounted in its broad teak surface was a half-sphere of crystal filled with clear liquid. Dawit Alta'ir slid open a door in the cabinet and took out a tablet and stylus.

"All right, Morningstar, you must show me what you can do. Draw me your kingdom."

"I haven't got a kingdom."

Dawit cuffed him lightly on the back of the head with the tablet. "You are the only child in this palace who hasn't, then," he said. "Aksum, you moonling. The kingdom you call home, your emperor's kingdom. Draw me Aksum."

Biting his lip at his own idiocy, Telemakos fixed the tablet firmly between his knees and pulled his mind into focus. He began to draw. He did not allow himself to grow absorbed, but he felt a faint glow of satisfaction as he guided the point of the stylus with surety across the beeswax plate.

Dawit Alta'ir reached forward to touch the plate, running light, quick fingertips over Telemakos's sketch.

"Neat work."

"Thank you, Magus."

"You manage your tools well," Dawit commented. "You and I shall be the blind leading the lame! I have a task you may begin today. I have not been able to do it myself, and I have been loath to entrust it to an untrained artist."

Dawit Alta'ir reached inside the cabinet again and began to take out tray after tray of inks and brushes, palm stalks covered with calculations, bone straight-edges, an abacus set, and an astrolabe in pieces. All of it was dust covered. He came to the tray he wanted and raised a small cloud blowing it clean. He and Telemakos choked together raspingly. Dawit set down the box, lifted from it one of two dozen small parcels bound in silk, and carefully removed the wrappings. Inside was yet another wax tablet made of four wooden blocks bound together with leather. Dawit opened them out like a screen and laid them across his knees.

"Can you see the map?" he asked.

Telemakos had to tilt his head this way and that to catch

the faintly scratched lines. Some had been smeared or had melted back into the wax. Abreha's lion-and-star seal was imprinted in the corner.

"Where is this?"

"That is of no consequence to you. What you are to do is to copy it, permanently, onto papyrus. I cannot see well enough to do it myself, and I dare not feel the original for fear of destroying it. Can you do such a thing?"

"I'll try."

"If your first draft is not good enough, make another. Every map in this box needs to be copied. Let us set out your workplace."

With no more fuss than that, Telemakos was apprenticed. The astronomer sat next to him, apparently watching his movements, but Telemakos thought Dawit probably could not make out the detail of the drawing. He wondered who would check the task for accuracy.

Dawit interrogated him as he drew.

"Now tell me, Medraut's son, what have you read? I take it for granted you are not one of those who believes that anyone who can predict star showers or an eclipse must be a sorcerer. Your father is an educated man. I met him in Aksum, fifteen years ago, when he was very young. He had a great collection of books that he had taken away from the Academy in Athens when Justinian closed it and sent the scholars packing. Have you read your father's books?"

"They were all destroyed before I could read," Telemakos

answered, frowning over the blurred scratches he was supposed to copy. "They were burnt with my grandfather's estate, in Britain, after the battle of Camlan."

The astronomer said contemptuously, "Kings, barbarians. Tell me what you've read that hasn't been burnt."

They worked together throughout the afternoon. When Athena's wailing began again, Dawit shouted down the hole in the floor, "Take that creature elsewhere!" After that, all was quiet on the floors below, and Telemakos wound himself in mathematics to avoid having to think about his abandoned lion and his abandoned sister.

At sundown the librarian brought them bowls of rice mixed with almonds and raisins, leaving them at the doorway as though this was routine. By the time they finished eating, they sat in darkness, but Dawit lit no lamp. A shaft of yellow light came up through the pulley hole.

Dawit crossed the floor. He did not touch the hanging crystals this time; their glitter allowed him to weave his way among them. He leaned over the shaft. His kat-stained beard glowed pale rose in the lemon light.

"Muna, all is very quiet down there."

Telemakos could hear Muna's answer as perfectly as if she were standing by his ear, clear but not loud.

"We have only just come up from the gardens. Rasha and I have taken all this day and a deal of physical abuse in trying to tempt this foundling to eat something, and I think it is only the opportunity to pour melted butter all down my dress that has driven her to take food from my hands. She is sitting here blinking and snorting, and in about a dozen seconds she will begin to bellow. Will it be you who spends the next hour singing her calm again while she tries to drag your hair from your scalp? My husband is home after three months, and I don't want him to find me doing battle with our new baby when he finally finishes his plotting and comes up to greet me."

As though they had awakened a sleeping monster, there came a wail and a rising roar from the room below.

"That baby is no foundling in any case," Dawit said. "She has father and mother at home, and has brought her brother with her. He will settle her. Bring her up here."

"I had not heard he was in San'a to learn to be a nursemaid."

"By my understanding he is an accomplished nursemaid already," Dawit threw down to his daughter. "He will soon put both of us out of work. Bring her up. I want to meet her. And you will like the boy."

At last Dawit Alta'ir lit a lamp. Telemakos wondered how long it had been since any light had been made in this room; he could smell the dust burning off in the new flame. Five minutes later Queen Muna stood in the doorway like the apparition of a genie, faintly glittering as the light caught her. Her gown and headscarf were sage green silk figured with darker green. She wore dozens of gold bracelets and a low tiara trimmed with gold bells, so that she rustled and jingled softly as she moved. Athena sobbed and trembled in her arms, her face buried in the queen's shoulder.

"Ah, my Muna," said Dawit softly. "Little mother."

Telemakos flew to take back his sister.

"Boy! Boy! Boy!" Athena choked, turning so quickly from Muna's shoulder to his that he did not ever see her red eyes or wet cheeks. He sat down with her on the bottom step. Her hair was plaited in elegant spirals around her head.

Muna picked her way down the steps around them and crouched, facing Telemakos. She ran her hand over Athena's plaits. "Better now, little girl? Ah, I can see that this is the one you love the best."

Athena looked up. Telemakos's heart gave a lurch when he saw her painted face. The spirals of her hair continued across her cheeks and forehead, in blue. Each line ended in pinpoint leaves and star-shaped flowers. It must have been done with a hairline paintbrush. It could not be the industrious work of the girl Inas.

Still sniveling a bit, Athena said to Muna, "Go away." Then she pointed to the ceiling and said, "Stars."

Telemakos bowed his head politely. "My lady Queen, your artistry is exquisite."

"Would I did so well as wife and mother," she answered sadly.

Telemakos glanced at her, hiding his curious gaze as he did habitually beneath his bent brow, and saw her Socotran eyes fixed on him. They were lighter than his own. They seemed green, like pale jade, but that could have been the reflection of her green gown. They might easily be blue or gray.

"Everything is strange to us here," Telemakos said. "Athena will learn to like it."

"They all do. I am mother to them all." There was the faintest hint of bitterness in her lovely voice. "But perhaps Athena would like to stay with you tonight."

She commented to the Star Master, "They're like their father, aren't they, Medraut's children. And like their kinsman Gwalchmei."

"I thought you'd see it," Dawit answered gruffly.

Dawit left the lamp burning when he escorted Muna downstairs to her husband's apartment. Athena stood among the silk rugs on Telemakos's mattress, gripping the curving stonework of the eastern windows, wavering unsteadily on her toes. She would not stand without support.

"Come, Tena, we can play now." Telemakos settled next to her. "Look at my cross staff. We can measure the angles to the Magus's hanging stars." Athena reached for it as he held it to his eye. "Wait."

He set his line of sight on Sirius, big and bright in the flickering lamplight, easy to read. Athena rattled the crosspiece back and forth along the staff.

"All right—slide that toward me. That's right—now stop. Stop!"

She snatched at the staff again, but not before Telemakos had read the angle.

"Well done, little Tena," he said softly, and let her have the crossed pieces of bone to play with. The water clock that crowned the pinnacle of the dome above them chimed the late hour; Telemakos blew out the lamp. Outside in the dark sky the real stars hung radiant. From the floor below came the faint twitter of the caged birds settling for the night, and from far-ther away, the floating sound of a single flute.

It is nice here, Telemakos thought, but everyone seems un-happy. Or discontented. I wonder what those maps are for, the maps I have to copy.

When Dawit Alta'ir wanted to chew kat, he threw his apprentice out among the orphaned Scions. Telemakos sat with them at lunch, beneath the songbirds, studying his most recent letter from Goewin while the little girls rolled oranges back and forth with Athena. She played amiably with the other children now and called them all by name. She called Muna and her companion Rasha by name as well. Telemakos had not heard Athena call anyone "mama" since they had left Adulis.

He was happy to let someone take over Athena's attention for the moment, because Goewin's letter puzzled him. It seemed to begin abruptly as though she were picking up a continuing conversation. The lion pit was being dug out to give Solomon and Sheba more room; Goewin described the work as though Telemakos already knew about it.

He had heard from her only twice before. Even allowing for the overland journey and the occasional post going astray, after three months and more in San'a, Telemakos thought it time Goewin's promised letters began to catch up with him. His father did not write to him either, but this did not surprise him. Letters arrived at least once a week from his mother, and it was already a month past Epiphany. Telemakos could not understand the lack of attention from Goewin. She had said she would write every week.

I wonder if someone opened this before it reached me, Telemakos thought, rereading Goewin's chatty tale of the emperor's lions for the fifth time. He could see the mark of her seal, but it had come off. He turned the page over and over, trying to find some hidden meaning in her odd, wrong-handed, spidery script.

Maybe someone is censoring her letters. Maybe that sunbird-killer is hoping to find intrigue in the British ambassador's messages. Maybe someone is taking her letters and keeping them.

Oh, Telemakos thought, I am safe out of it, but I am so far away. How can I warn Goewin of anything? It takes three months, a whole season, for her to write to me and receive an answer.

"Morningstar," said Shadi, the obedient young tribal king. Telemakos looked up and realized that Shadi was talking to him, and had said the name twice already. Dawit used it so freely that Muna and now the children had picked it up as well, but Telemakos was not used to it.

"How did you learn to move in such catfoot quiet?" Shadi asked. "You don't even make a noise turning the pages. I would not know you were here if I couldn't see you."

Telemakos laughed. "My father is quiet," he answered. "I must have learned from him. Sometimes he doesn't even bother to speak. He wouldn't have taken me hunting if I'd ever made a noise. I used to hunt with him, before my accident."

"You could hawk," Shadi said tactfully. "The najashi doesn't allow us weapons of any kind, but he has given me a sparrow-hawk."

Telemakos recognized, suddenly, a difference between these children and those of al-Muza: even the smallest boys in al-Muza had worn their curved wooden knives with pride, but Abreha's Royal Scions were daggerless.

"Why aren't you allowed weapons?" he asked.

"We are noble."

"Oh." Telemakos considered the possible reasoning behind this, and his own guess as to why no one at home would teach him to throw a spear. "Are you hostages?"

Shadi gave him a pitying, astonished look, as though he could not believe that even a crippled foreigner could be so ignorant. "Whose good faith would my well-being buy? My father and brothers are dead."

"That of your tribe, surely?"

"My clansmen, my limbs, shed blood in my name, not I in

theirs. I am their head. A sovereign must learn to govern, to direct, not to wield arms."

What about me? Telemakos wondered. Does Abreha consider me, as well, too noble to bear a weapon? I haven't a kingdom to govern; I'm nothing to Himyar. I'm going to ask Abreha for a spear. The sling's all right for birds, but I have got to find a way to hunt properly again.

Athena sat curled against her brother's thigh, fitting lozenges of colored paint into a partitioned tray. She played nearly as often in the Globe Room as in the nursery, and as long as she was busy she did not try to destroy precious instruments or documents. Dawit Alta'ir was remarkably tolerant of her. He let Athena play with his hair and pick the leaves out of his beard and sort the semiprecious stones he used to make his globes.

The king had come up to see Telemakos at work, and watched from over his shoulder. "I do not remember a request that all our maps be illuminated, Dawit Cartographer," Abreha said.

Telemakos had decorated the blank edges of the page he was working on. A line of pelicans flew across the top of the sheet; flamingoes stalked its lower corners.

"The Morningstar does that. It keeps the fuss to a minimum. Athena likes to watch her brother draw."

"What is he working at?"

"Copying the plague tablets."

"Does he know what they represent?"

"I have not told him."

"I do not wish these plans to leave this library."

"Send me another who can do the work adequately, and I will use him instead."

Have they forgotten I am here? Telemakos wondered. He said lightly, "You are making me curious."

"That is a fair warning," Abreha acknowledged. He watched in silence for a time. Then he sat back on his heels and said at last, "Your master's named you well, Athtar the Morningstar, the Bright One."

Telemakos kept working, stiffly, and said nothing. Goewin's twin brother, Lleu, the lost prince of Britain, had also been named "Bright One." It made Telemakos feel ghost-touched to be compared to his dead uncle.

The paintbrush slipped from Telemakos's fingers and spattered ink across the pelicans at the top of the page.

"Do not scold, Dawit," the najashi said quickly, before the Star Master could open his mouth. "I am interfering with your student's concentration."

"Oh? Then it is something I can't see. What has he done?"

"Spilt ink everywhere," Telemakos said, blowing on the spots to dry them. Suddenly, with a purposeful change of direction, the najashi crouched low beside Athena. Crow's feet creased the taut edges of his temples. Beneath his heavy brow, his rare smile was sweet and open.

"Little honey badger, do you remember me? You may come and play with the paints in my study anytime you like. I'll have

Muna bring you down, and your brother may be spared your attention now and again."

Athena gave him a paint block.

"The king's gratitude to you, my lovely."

Athena pointed to his ring. She stared openly into his face with her wide gray eyes; no one had taught her that it was impolite to gaze directly at a king. Telemakos swallowed a sigh. That was probably his fault.

"See lion," Athena said.

"Yes, that is my father's ring," Abreha said. He twisted the signet into his palm, to tease her. "Gone."

"Lion!"

Abreha turned the ring back around his finger. "Here it is."

"See Tena's lion," Athena explained more specifically, and gave the najashi's ancient family crest a derisive smack. "Baby lion." She turned the tray of ink blocks upside down. They clattered over Telemakos's work in a cloud of color and dust, and the baby crawled into Abreha's lap. "See Tena's lion, najashi!" she said.

Telemakos felt his heart turn over with a thump of astonishment and envy. *She can say najashi! It's almost as long as Telemakos, and it isn't even her first language! Why am I still Boy?*

"That was her first full sentence," Telemakos said. "You had better indulge her."

Abreha laughed with ringing joy. "Now we know the way to your heart, little honey badger! Well, that is what I in truth have come for, to request the boy's assistance with my lion, and if you will let me carry you, you may come, too. I want to take your apprentice away early today, Dawit. Menelik behaves much better for Telemakos than for me."

"Take care with his one arm, playing with lions," Dawit said grudgingly, "or you will never get your maps copied."

Menelik was proving to be considerably more difficult to train than a dog. Telemakos secretly thought the lion more intelligent than the gazelle hounds, because, like most cats, it refused to perform without good reason. Telemakos never spoke this suspicion aloud. The salukis were nearly sacred: owned strictly by nobility, so prized and honored they could never be sold, only given as gifts. Telemakos longed for one of his own.

On this afternoon, Menelik performed with typical dis-obedience. He would not retrieve a dead pigeon; he guarded it selfishly in a corner of the yard until Telemakos had to go and wrestle it away from him. He came when Telemakos called him, but not when anybody else did. Athena could get him to run in the right direction if she scampered ahead of him on all fours, growling and chirping in lion language. They tussled over the pigeon, which Athena was intrigued by; she could not understand a bird that did not move. The animal keepers loved the way she fooled with the lion, but Telemakos did not. Athena might think she was a lion cub, but what did Menelik think she was?

"He will only be a nuisance to your gazelle hounds in the chase," Telemakos told Abreha, who watched his experiment unfold with great interest. "Menelik will never be as fast as they are, and I don't think he can sight as well."

"He is ready to learn to hunt," said Abreha. "He has the strength. He has the instinct."

"His mother is supposed to teach him. And then he is supposed to let his wife do most of the work."

Abreha laughed. "He thinks you are his mother. You will have to come along and show him what to do."

After an hour of this hard play, the najashi held Athena up so they could watch Telemakos and the keepers drilling some small sense of discipline into Menelik, who had at least learned to stop and wait when told. When Telemakos next looked over, Athena had fallen asleep in Abreha's arms, her head on his shoulder and the side of her face pressed against the beadwork of his robe.

The najashi was scowling, but it was the curse of his heavy brow that he always seemed unhappy. He held the baby so easily, so gently. Oh, Telemakos thought with a surge of sadness, how I wish, how I wish my father had held her like that.

Abreha carried Athena back up through the staircases. Telemakos followed, watching his sister's head bobbing over the najashi's shoulder. She slept, oblivious to her changing surroundings. It was a relief to Telemakos, for once, not to have to carry her up the stairs himself. I suppose she won't be able to come along when we take Menelik out in the wild, he thought. You can't take your baby sister hunting with you. Ras Meder might argue I shouldn't go, either, if he knew.

Telemakos remembered the question he wanted to put to Abreha.

"Will you teach me to throw a spear?"

Abreha continued up the stairs and did not answer immediately, but at the next landing, without turning around, he asked, "Why?"

"You said I might hunt with you. I cannot use a bow."

"Come hunting with the salukis before you prepare for war," Abreha said. "Perhaps you'll find you do not need a spear. A sunbird has no sting, but it may hang its nest near a hive and let the hornets protect its young."

Telemakos missed the next step and fell halfway back down the flight.

"Mother of God, boy! Are you hurt?"

"I am not—" Telemakos coughed, and with all the terror and falseness of Peter denying his condemned teacher, cried out, "I am not a sunbird!"

He thought he was going to fall farther, and scrabbled at the steps with heels and knees, half expecting the worn marble floors of the Ghumdan palaces to turn to salt and sand beneath him.

"Are you trying to fly? I did not mean it literally!" The najashi made his way carefully down to Telemakos, still cradling Athena over his left shoulder, his right hand held out in an offer of concern. He crouched against the stair wall and pulled Telemakos's shamma aside, searching him for injury. His touch was gentle and careful. *Are you hurt?*

"I'm all right," Telemakos said, subduing himself.

"Thank heaven you were not carrying the baby!"

Telemakos rubbed his shins. "I lose my balance easily. I have not got used to being lopsided."

"Your father made note of that in the instruction he sent concerning your wounds, and I have noticed it myself, watching you play with the lion. You used to move like a fox, quick and quiet. You are more cautious now."

Athena stirred, muttering about the poor bird. She meant Menelik's pigeon.

Abreha let go of Telemakos so that he could settle the baby more comfortably. He backed down the stairs, holding Athena firm in one arm, and helped Telemakos to his feet with the other. "Perhaps you do need a soldier's training. We might be able to drill your poise back into you. Well, a light javelin would suit you, Telemakos Morningstar. We will fit you with a dart of some kind. As you say, you are not a sunbird."

Telemakos touched the whitewashed wall to steady himself. He managed to speak with level gratitude. "Thank you, my najashi. I would pledge such a weapon to your service."

"Withhold your pledge awhile," Abreha said. "When you've learned to use such a weapon, I'll remind you of your offer."

"And," the najashi added thoughtfully, "Tharan will train you to ride like a desert soldier. All the best spearmen ride. You may find it difficult at first. Tharan always makes the cadets start off blindfolded."

XIII

TAMING THE LION

TELEMAKOS STARED AT the abacus before him. He covered his eyes, held them closed, and uncovered them. He could do it himself without shuddering. He covered them again. When he looked at the abacus, he could not remember what he had been figuring.

I used to practice, he remembered. I was going to cross the pool in the lion pit with my shamma over my face, but then Solomon tried to eat me.

"Magus," Telemakos said to Dawit, "however long I stare, these clear glass beads trick me like fury. Could I learn to count them by touch, the way you do?"

Dawit said indifferently, "Close your eyes and try it."

"Tape them shut, so I don't cheat," Telemakos said.

Dawit unwrapped his sash and held it up. It was of heavy silk, dark blue, the ends decorated with trees embroidered in copper thread. "Come, then."

It's all right, it's all right, Telemakos told himself, if I can do this here, I can do it tomorrow morning on the training ground.

But when the rough silk touched his eyelids, Telemakos fought like a cornered leopard.

Dawit did not draw back in dismayed concern like everyone else. He held on, and pulled the silk tight. Beneath the astronomer's robes, his long limbs were strong as iron bands; he was taller and heavier than Telemakos, but his chief advantage was that he wrestled purposefully, while Telemakos struggled without knowing where he was or who he was fighting.

Dawit overpowered him. When Telemakos came to his senses, he was lying on his back on the floor, with the broken abacus beneath him, scattered beads pressing into his shoulders and spine. Dawit's sash was fixed firmly over his eyes and crossed down around his neck. Dawit held him still, gripping the ends of the sash on either side of Telemakos's throat, poised to subdue him further.

"Did you fight like that the first time they did this to you?"

He had not fought at all. He had let them do it. His life had depended on his willing obedience. It was a question Telemakos could not answer. He choked back a sob, twisting his head aside to try to work it free.

"You must know you cannot bear such treatment. Why did you ask me to do it?"

Telemakos hiccupped.

"Breathe," Dawit told him. "I will hold you here until you explain yourself in a rational manner."

"I am—" Telemakos swallowed, and managed to croak, "I wanted to practice. Tharan is to give me riding lessons, and the najashi says I must be blindfolded to improve my balance—" He broke off with a sharp cry, struggling again like a bird in a snare.

"Eh," Dawit grunted. "You are a deal more damaged than you let on, and it was not all done by wild beasts. Were you sequestered? Or punished for seeing something you shouldn't have? Or just tormented by other boys? Well, I see why you want to practice. I'll help you, if you allow it. Turn around so I can tie this fast."

He rolled Telemakos over beneath him and fixed the sash in a tight knot behind his head. Telemakos cringed, sobbing.

"Get up and stop quaking. Give me your hand."

He helped Telemakos to his feet and guided him to one of the hanging stars. Telemakos closed his fingers around cold quartz and silver wire.

"Tell me its name," Dawit ordered.

Telemakos stifled another sob. "How?" he gasped.

"You must find it out."

Telemakos took a tentative step forward, holding on to the crystal star on its cotton thread. It was a small one. He found another quite close to it, took hold of the second, and let go of the first. Since the execution at al-Muza he had dreamed of scorpions but not of Hara.

"Lesath? The sting?"

"You're guessing. Concentrate; it is only a task, a lesson you must complete."

Telemakos thought about stars. He remembered how it had made him cry, to see them again after three months. Dawit would never see them at all anymore. Telemakos stepped sideways and found a third hanging crystal. He stood clinging to it, the wire cutting into the inside of his fingers. He tossed his head, as though he could shake free of the binding.

"*Think*," the Star Master ordered. "You are not a horse, to shy at shadows and flags in the wind."

Telemakos ground his teeth together in determination and paced out a purposeful plot of nine stars.

"The Hunter," he said at last. "The first star was Mintaka."

"Damnably well done. Come back to Rigel," Dawit commanded. Telemakos made his way across the constellation, and Dawit met him. He untied the blindfold.

Telemakos sighed, simply grateful for the reprieve.

"Take the sash," Dawit said. "Bind it on yourself this time, and find me the Polestar."

Think about the stars, Telemakos told himself.

He gripped one end of the cloth in his teeth and wound the sash around his head. *The Polestar.* He tucked fast the leftover measure of silk. *Think. You are not a horse.* He caught hold of the nearest star and drew a deep breath.

"It's easier when I do it myself," he said.

"Do it yourself tomorrow."

"They'll want to be sure it's tight."

"Come here, then."

Dawit was brutal. His long, bony fingers were quick and strong, and he would not allow Telemakos to flinch. When Telemakos wailed in desperation, "Too tight!" Dawit struck him a jarring clip across the face with the flat of his hand.

"Do you see, son of Medraut, this is how they will do it. They are used to training soldiers. They will tolerate no softness in you, and show none themselves."

He pulled the sash free. Telemakos had time to draw one long, ragged breath before Dawit caught him from behind with one arm holding him fast by the shoulders and the other hand clapped over his eyes, blinding him again. Telemakos let out a shriek.

"*Mother of God.*" Dawit spat in disgust. He let go of Telemakos's eyes, let him draw another convulsive breath, and covered his eyes again. When Telemakos at last managed to bear this treatment without struggling or crying out, Dawit once more bound his sash across Telemakos's face.

They kept at this torturous exercise for so long that it grew dark and Telemakos did not know it.

By and by there was a clamor in the scriptorium. Telemakos, blindfolded, heard Dawit go to the door to look.

"Come and see, Morningstar," Dawit said. Telemakos pushed the sash back from his face. The blue silk was damp with his tears and sweat. He climbed the three stairs to the upper reading room.

Three of the Scions and Athena were approaching the Great Globe Room. Shadi led the way, reluctantly, glancing over his shoulder at the laughing and chattering girls; Inas and Malika each had Athena by one hand, encouraging her to walk between them.

"Tena swing," Telemakos heard his sister ordering in South Arabian. "Swing Tena up."

"Not in the library, dumpling," Inas said. "Look, there's your brother!"

"Has he learned anything yet, do you think?" asked Malika, and laughed at her own joke.

"Come and see," Dawit told them. "Make a light, Shadi. My apprentice is inconvenienced by flint and tinder."

He lined the girls up, side by side, on the cushions beneath the east window. Malika hooked one arm around Athena's middle to keep her still, while the Star Master spread a chart in Inas's lap. "Bring the lamp here, Shadi. Inas, can you read the names? Good. Find the Polestar. There, in the center." He stabbed a blind finger into the page at random. "When I give the word, you shall call out a name—pick those not too far off—and we shall see if the Morningstar can find them. Shadi!"

Shadi jumped. The lamp flickered. "Yes, Magus?"

"Blindfold your friend."

Telemakos stood still. Shadi set the lamp on the windowsill, then came up behind Telemakos and fumbled to pull the sash down over his eyes. The hated cloth against Telemakos's eyelids made his skin prick with horror, as always, but Telemakos knew it was Shadi doing it, and where he was, and why. It was no worse than getting dressed each morning. Telemakos did not shudder or make any kind of noise.

Thank God, he thought with fierce joy.

Dawit guided him to take hold of a quartz star. Telemakos said aloud, "*Thank you,* Magus."

Malika was only faintly impressed that Telemakos could hunt his way across the Globe Room blindfolded. "That is what you're here for, isn't it?" she said dismissively. "To learn to map the sky? Show us something worth seeing."

Telemakos turned in the direction of her voice.

"Line up," he ordered. "The three of you, Malika, Inas, Shadi. Get in line one behind the other. Then come and stand in front of me and I'll guess which of you it is."

Before his accident Telemakos had been a superb tracker. These three were easy to tell by their scent alone: Inas with indigo-stained fingers, Malika with attar of jasmine in her hair, Shadi having spent the afternoon in the mews with his sparrowhawk. Telemakos could sense Athena watching from the sofa, quiet and interested, smelling of sandalwood.

They could not work out how he told them apart. He was so unerring in his identification of them, even when they approached him from behind, or switched places with one another at the last second, that they thought he must be cheating. Malika insisted they wrap Shadi's sash over top of Dawit's.

"Go on, then," Telemakos said, kneeling so she could

reach. "Only spare my nose and mouth, so I can breathe."

"Enough, boy," Dawit said gently.

"It is a game," Telemakos answered stubbornly. "I can do it."

He was sweating and trembling when at last he felt his way to the window and let Athena pull his head free of its various bindings. The others all came piling in around him. Telemakos, giddy with triumph and relief, let Inas and Malika tumble over him as they tried to get Shadi's sash away from Athena. Inas started to tickle her, and Athena screamed with laughter.

"*Behave*," Dawit barked suddenly. "Inas of Ma'in. You are too old for such foolishness." He moved swiftly in the lamp-cast shadows, sure of himself. "Are you short of entertainment, like street children at a beheading? Sit still and be quiet, and I will show you my sky map."

He began to fill the largest of his lamps, which Telemakos had never seen alight, with clear oil. The lamp held five wicks in glass globes, which were cased in a great surround of thick lenses. Like all the Star Master's lamps, it was coated with dust, and Dawit wiped the outside of the glass quickly with his sleeve. "Shadi, light these, then sit. All of you attend."

The big lamp made the room brighter than it was at any time except early morning, when the sunlight flared directly through the windows.

The Star Master strode purposefully to the pulley in the corner. With one long, rattling tug on the chain and weights, he lowered the Great Globe. Dawit unhooked a catch on the side of the globe, opened a hinged panel in its dark, speckled surface, and carefully set the five-flamed lamp inside. He closed the door. The globe became a sparkling orb of pinpoint lights.

"I can't see this anymore, but it is time the Morningstar made some use of it." He paced back across the room to give another long tug on the pulley. "Put out the little lamp, Inas."

The stars rose, and the domed black ceiling suddenly mirrored the night sky. Dawit put a hand on the globe and spun it slowly, and the stars turned.

"Your crystals are in the way," Telemakos said. "They catch the light and glitter—"

The room was utterly bewitching in its beauty.

"I cannot see," said the astronomer. "I can see the light catching the crystals, but not the soft lights against the dome above. The crystals can be fixed against the ceiling so they are out of the way. We'll do that tomorrow." Dawit gave a great push to the side of the globe, using both hands, and the stars wheeled at a dizzying pace.

Malika gasped. Athena shouted, "Again! Again!" She pulled herself up to stand behind Telemakos with her arms locked around his neck, watching the show from over his shoulder. Telemakos sat with Shadi pressing against one side of him and Inas against the other, while Athena leaned over his back, cheek to cheek with him. Never in his life had Telemakos felt so loved, and so at ease, with others more or less his own age. He had not missed it; he had never known life could be like this. And now he was ready to learn to hunt.

Telemakos thought, not for the first time, I am glad to be here.

He did not flinch when Tharan bound fast his eyes in the training ring the next morning. The neat desert horse he was to ride was whickering near his shoulder, and Telemakos, drawn by its warm smell of sun and dung, reached up blind to fondle its bony head and rub its coarse-silk cheek against his own. When Tharan helped him up and Telemakos sat astride the narrow back, gripping the saddle cloth behind him, he wondered briefly, What am I to these people? I am not a hostage. I am not a servant. Abreha can't expect me to repay him for any of his gifts. Why are they teaching me such *mastery*?

He wondered only briefly. He did not care. He had never expected anyone to give him a warrior's training, and he was too grateful to question it.

Daily after that, at daybreak, Telemakos joined the palace guard in their target practice. The cadets were all at least a year older than he, so even if he had been whole as the rest of them, he would not have been expected to achieve their standards. But Telemakos was never treated with any kind of indulgence. The vizier Tharan directed them in this as well, and he was a hard taskmaster. But he approached the challenge of uncovering the most effective technique for a one-armed warrior as though it was the most fascinating puzzle he had ever been set. Telemakos, slowly acquiring some skill, did not mind the work.

He thought of hunting with his father in years to come and was driven with hope.

One morning when Telemakos came through the library on his way back to the Globe Room after his daily practice, he found the custodian carefully copying a list of royal transactions of olive oil. Supervising this work, of all men, was the merchant Gedar, Grandfather's neighbor from the villa across the street to the house of Nebir.

"Peace to you, Telemakos Meder," Gedar greeted him, smiling. "Are you surprised to find me here?"

Telemakos knelt, swiftly and sincerely, and bowed his head. My poise is coming back, he thought; I must thank Tharan for his attention.

Telemakos apologized to Gedar. "Of course I know you traffic with the Himyar court."

"Indeed, I was sent as a messenger again," Gedar said. "I am in San'a on business, but your family have given me letters to deliver you."

"Oh, thank you, sir!"

"Come, sit by me."

Telemakos obeyed eagerly—too eagerly, for Gedar's expression changed. He warned, "You'll be disappointed. They are badly sea-damaged; our crossing was nearly unendurable." He handed over to Telemakos a wallet of woven raffia, warped and stained with salt. Telemakos bent over the packet and knew, even before he opened it, that the letters within would be unreadable. The pages fell to shreds when he tried to pull them out.

He wiped the pulp from his fingertips against the outside of the folder, feeling suddenly desolate. He longed for another letter from Goewin.

"What filthy bad luck," Harith the librarian said sympathetically.

"It was base neglect on my part, not luck," Gedar said. "I am sorry, Telemakos. I should have kept them with my invoices. They would have survived in my document case." He reached for the hide-bound box resting on the floor beside him. "You see." He laid open the lid. Paper and parchment scrolls lay packed in dry ranks like rows of bone. Telemakos smelled dust and faint decay.

It was like a blow to the skull. For a long moment he had to sit very still, holding his head against his knees, sick with what that breath brought to his memory: the bright green plumage of the murdered sunbird, the nail through its back.

Telemakos raised his head.

"I'm sorry," Gedar said again.

His whole house smelled like that, Telemakos remembered. God help me, I do not dream when Athena is there by me, I can ride a horse and carry a spear blindfolded, Afar is on the other side of the Red Sea and Hara is dead. And yet still the smell of dust makes me faint?

"It can't be helped," Telemakos replied quietly.

◆　◆　◆

Gedar, as the najashi's guest, was invited along to view the parkland beyond the blossoming almond groves north of the city,
the very first time the lion Menelik was taken out to hunt with
the gazelle hounds. The hunting party was small, only seven
men and four dogs. Gedar stuck by Telemakos, though clear of
the lion, of which Telemakos had charge. The olive merchant's
endless questions of polite interest quickly wore Telemakos's
patience thin. The thought of setting the lion loose was making him increasingly nervous, even without Gedar distracting
him; he knew that neither he nor Menelik was ready for this.

Menelik startled at everything, at insects, at nodding
leaves, at birdcalls. It became such a struggle to contain him
that Telemakos had to give up the two short lances strapped
over his back. It was his first time bearing weapons any distance, and he was not yet comfortable or familiar enough with
their weight to carry them and keep fast Menelik's lead.

"I should take him home," Telemakos said apologetically.
Abreha held the lion while Telemakos, burning with humilia-
tion at having to admit to weakness before half a dozen courtiers, turned his spears over to Gedar.

"The lion is not your responsibility," said Abreha. "He is
mine. Have no fear, we will not run him today. It will do him no
harm to see the salukis in action. Will you take him again?"

"Do you trust me?" Telemakos asked miserably.

"What a question, Morningstar. Would I tempt you to prove
yourself if I did not?"

"You might do it as a test of my judgment."

"You are a prudent judge," said Abreha. "Yes, I trust you."

Telemakos eyed Abreha's dogs with disloyal envy. White Nech and ruddy gold Werkama strutted unleashed at the najashi's side, reliable in their obedience. They held their long ears raised and alert, their feathered tails high. Every so often Nech trotted close to Menelik and nosed at him in concerned interest. I would sell my soul to call one of these dogs my own, Telemakos thought for the hundredth time.

Within the thorn boundary of the royal parkland, the hounds galloped away. They doubled back almost immediately, tongues out in wide, glorious smiles, and settled into a trot ahead of Abreha and his men.

"Watch," the najashi said to Gedar. "Werkama has one."

The najashi clapped his hands suddenly, and all four dogs were gone. Telemakos missed seeing them go. Menelik had lunged forward at the command, and Telemakos scolded him and dragged him back. He thought the lead was going to sever his fingers.

"Not yet!"

He seized the lion by the ear and sat on him.

"If you don't behave, I will never run with you again," Telemakos told him fiercely. "You are going to outweigh me in about one month. If you want to come hunting, you will have to go with someone heavier, or *hold!*"

Menelik growled, but with frustration and not at Telemakos.

The other men moved forward in the direction of the dogs, scanning the rise ahead for the antelope they had started after.

"There," said one, and pointed. Werkama and Nech reappeared out of the nearest hollow and flew slantwise over the next rise, followed by their companions. The dogs' sleek, long bodies were stretched nearly linear; their feathered tails moved in unison as rudders. The reedbuck ahead of them was a yellow streak, but Telemakos saw how easily they would cut it off together, two from either side. The racing creatures disappeared like wind over the crest of the hill.

"On horseback a man may follow the chase," the najashi commented for Gedar's benefit, "but we'll have no chance afoot. They'll be waiting for us with their catch when we arrive."

They set out toward the jagged al-Surat Mountains that rimmed the plateau. Abreha himself set them on the slight trail the hounds and reedbuck had left, but he let Menelik and Telemakos lead them. The lion was almost pathetically eager to please now, as if he knew he were somehow inferior to his canine companions. Telemakos caught the scent of fresh blood before Menelik did, but no one was likely to notice that.

The dogs were lying proudly alert alongside their prize when Abreha's party found them half an hour later. The lion grew so excited that it took Telemakos and Abreha together to wrestle him into compliance.

"My najashi—" Telemakos gasped. "My najashi, this is *foolhardy*. Let me take him home."

"Will you manage him on your own?"

"Away from this kill, yes."

Abreha conceded. "Now he knows how it is done. We'll take him with us again soon, and unleash him. I am not discouraged yet."

Menelik was still whining and trembling when he and Telemakos reached the kennels. Telemakos leaned against the rails and watched the animal keepers feed him, but the lion would not allow himself to be rubbed and brushed as the dogs did, so after a time the keepers left him alone in his pen to recover himself. But Telemakos could not leave him. He slipped through the slats of the lion's pen and chirped softly to his friend.

Menelik crawled close to Telemakos and reached to touch his leg with one padded paw, softly as a falling leaf and with his claws perfectly sheathed, begging for comfort as desperately as Athena did. He pushed the top of his heavy head against Telemakos's chin, demanding kisses.

"Oh, you are such a baby," Telemakos whispered, and lay down beside the young lion, burrowing beneath the straw. It was warm, and smelled faintly of stale honey, like Menelik's fur. *I'll stay here till he sleeps,* Telemakos thought. *He, too, was tired to the bone,* but too wary of the lion's mood to allow himself to fall asleep there. He lay still, resting his body, listening with interest to the sounds of the kennel. Already he could tell five of the dogs by their voices.

That is Werkama. Abreha must be back.

Telemakos listened as the kennelmen took care of the

hunting dogs. He heard someone make a report to Abreha on the condition of the lion, and Abreha thanked his servants and dismissed them.

Which is the dog that won't stop crying? Telemakos wondered. That's not one of the hunters. That is a half-grown pup complaining for milk—

"Hush, hush, my bold, brave girl," said Abreha's voice. "Gedar will take care of you—"

The whining stopped.

"—for a time, and when he brings you to Aksum, my cousin Gebre Meskal will be your new family."

"It is a generous gift, Mukarrib," said Gedar.

How pompous Gedar is, Telemakos thought. No one calls Abreha "federator" unless it is in a formal ceremony.

"An easy gift. My cousin grows mistrustful of me, and this is one small way to mollify his suspicions."

They think they are alone, Telemakos realized. The lion is asleep and the kennelmen have been sent away. They don't know I'm here.

"What message shall I bring your cousin?" Gedar asked.

"Oh, no message, only the gift. I do not want to raise the Aksumite emperor's hackles with empty words."

"Your wish is my command," Gedar answered Abreha with obsequious humility. "I am your servant."

Telemakos grinned, listening eagerly, too practiced an eavesdropper to make any noise. This was wonderful luck.

He should have guessed there was more to Gedar than met the eye.

"Listen then," Abreha answered him, speaking low and quickly. "I will tell it once only. Send no more of your cryptic carrion threats, all those foul dead birds, to Gebre Meskal or his counselor Kidane; my vizier is sure now that Kidane is not the man we seek, and you begin to risk yourself. I do not like such underhand methods in any case. We will flush out the emperor's spies some other way."

Telemakos lay flat in the lion's straw, his light breath muffled by Menelik's purring snorts. Unease and disbelief began to crowd his spirit like circling vultures.

"Grind to pieces any amole salt you have kept from before the new year, for you must not cast abroad any hint you had exchange with Himyar during Gebre Meskal's quarantine. I will make good your loss."

Oh, my najashi, go away. Go away. I don't want to hear this. I don't want to know.

"It is all quite old," said Gedar. "I received nothing after the emperor shut down the operation in the Salt Desert. How he managed to break that apart is still a mystery."

"He had an informer there."

The pup began to whine again.

"Ah, the elusive sunbird; the scourge of Afar. The voice crying in the wilderness."

Oh, my najashi.

Telemakos had never known such betrayal. His heartbeat, fast and furious in his ears, was not loud enough to stifle the sound of Abreha's voice, relentlessly continuing this unbearable, unbelievable conversation.

"Sunbird is an old name; they no longer use it."

"What did the Scorpion tell you?" Gedar asked.

"Many contradictory stories," said Abreha quietly, "and few of them seem true. Hara was desperate, and a liar, and knew that I was making an example of him for Gebre Meskal's benefit. Oh, he was guilty of every last thing we accused him of, but there was betrayal of our contract on my part as well as his, and he defied and denied me at the end as far as he was able."

"Ah well," said Gedar. "How Gebre Meskal unraveled the enterprise in Afar is of little matter now his quarantine is lifted."

"Still, I should like to know who or what his link was there, and if he will strike against us with the same weapon another day. Anako, the one we called Lazarus, might know more, but he will remain Gebre Meskal's prisoner until the Hanish Islands are mine. When I went to the archipelago to escape the plague in al-Muza, I was never able to set foot on al-Kabir, the fortress island. I cannot land my soldiers there without being sure of a water supply and a defensible place to make camp. But if we cannot take the islands from without, maybe we can take them from within. If you see to it that a year from now my agents have infiltrated Gebre Meskal's navy, I will by then have better maps of the archipelago, and we can attempt a mutiny."

Serpent! Serpent! Serpent!

Telemakos listened to the sounds of them putting the pup back with its mother. The crying began again, briefly, then stopped; the dog would stay with the rest of the pack until Gedar went home.

"See what more you can learn from the boy," Abreha finished. "I'll send for him to dine alone with us tonight. It will be appropriate, after our quest today, and you are neighbors in your own land. Engage him in talk of his father; he thirsts for word of his family. I shall turn the talk to my will."

Your will be damned, Telemakos fumed, his throat constricted with fury and betrayal. *Serpent!* I will give you nothing. I will give you less than nothing.

Through his anger, fear brushed Telemakos's spine like fine, cold mist.

I have got to be upstairs before the najashi sends for me.

He managed it. He followed Abreha and Gedar into the palace, slipping soundlessly past them when they stopped to discuss the day's hunt with Tharan in the steward's reception hall. Telemakos took the steps two at a time the whole way up to the children's room.

"You might have come earlier," said Inas, with good nature. "Your sister has not yet managed to scream herself unconscious, nor eaten anything all day. Queen Muna is looking for you. The najashi sent you some opium."

Telemakos stared at her blankly, panting. The caged birds chattered and fluted over their heads.

"Why?" he managed at last. His throat was raw with the exertion of climbing twelve flights of stairs at racing speed.

"Shouldn't you know?" Inas asked in surprise.

"It is because you were hunting today, and they expect you to be all stiff and sore," put in Malika. "They like to fuss over you. Remember the night you fell down the stairs?" She gazed at Telemakos with interest. "You certainly don't look very happy. Your face is all tear streaked and you haven't even bothered to wipe it off. Do they give you opium only when they think you need it, or can you ask for it whenever you like?"

"Whenever I like," Telemakos said hoarsely, and stalked past them. Athena was in the nursery, sitting on the floor facing Muna and refusing to eat. She saw Telemakos and turned her bowl over.

"Boy! Boy! Tena's Boy!" She scrambled over to clutch at his legs, looking up at him adoringly.

Muna glanced up as well. For a moment her uncanny eyes met his. Telemakos peeled Athena away from his legs so he could kneel before the queen. He bent his head, still breathing hard.

"I beg your pardon, my lady Queen."

"You must stop hurling yourself about," Muna said gently. "We should all like to see you come to manhood without further adventure."

From one rustling silk sleeve she pulled a slender silver tube and held it out to him. "You are to use this at your discretion, as your father instructed you."

Telemakos hesitated, still trembling with outrage and bewilderment and sheer physical exhaustion. He generally refused the offer of opium. He parted his lips to make another polite objection, but it suddenly occurred to him he ought to make a dutiful pretense, at least, of clouding his brain. It might be to his advantage if Abreha imagined his guard was lowered.

"Thank you," Telemakos said, and took the case, wondering how to get rid of it.

Muna's friend and handmaid Rasha stood at the door.

"The najashi requests the Morningstar to share his meal tonight," she said. "Tharan Vizier is here to escort you."

This is happening too quickly, Telemakos thought. I know too much. I haven't thought any of it through. I need a shield.

Athena still clamored at his side. "Up! Up!"

Her saddle was hanging on one of a row of hooks by the door. Telemakos stood up and tucked the vial of opium inside it, where he had also hidden an unopened parcel of powder given him the day he had taken a fall during his riding lesson.

"Will she try to get at that?" Muna asked.

"She can't reach it. This pocket is mine. It's inside the other, and seals." He squatted on his heels beside Athena, pulling on the leather sleeve and lifting the shoulder strap over his head.

"She has not eaten," Muna warned.

"The najashi will find something to tempt her with."

"He will send her back up here, if he means to share a formal meal with his guest."

Athena climbed willingly into her saddle without being prompted.

"She has him enchanted," Telemakos said. "She sits in his study every morning while I am riding, and plays with his ink brushes." He buckled his sister against him and looked up. Muna's mouth was set in the hard, pursed grimace of someone who is biting back tears; her pale green eyes were too bright. Telemakos took her hand, quickly, and bent to rub noses with her, as the Himyarites did in greeting.

"I will bring Athena back soon, sweet lady, and in a better temper."

"Stop here a moment, Morningstar," Muna said. "You look as though you have been weeping." She pushed the pale hair back from his temples with cool, dry hands. "Now stay still until you stop gasping and can breathe again."

Telemakos waited. Muna gave her shy, sad smile and took her hands away.

"There. Now you are ready. Rasha, please warn Tharan that the boy has not yet used the anodyne, and has not washed."

XIV

THE COVENANT

THARAN LED TELEMAKOS down the narrow flights. He made no comment about Athena, who was taking on and off two of Muna's bangles that were tied to her saddle.

"Did you use your spear today?"

"I couldn't," Telemakos said.

"Did no chance arise?"

"I wasn't able to manage a weapon and the lion together," Telemakos admitted in a low voice.

"Better fortune next time out," Tharan said, offering neither praise nor blame. "You must try a hunt on horseback, soon, as well."

Tharan led them to the najashi's own apartment, a sprawling suite of luxurious chambers and terraces on one of the palace's middle stories. There were guards outside the door, but the rooms were empty. No life stirred in them except the flames in the brass sconces. There was not even a birdcage. All was bright and quiet.

"The najashi and his guest are still in the bathhouse," Tharan said. "They will be here presently. Wash your face at the basin in the antechamber. There's wine heating on the brazier in the study; I will leave a cup for you on the writing table, and you may administer your potions as you see fit. I must see to the attendants now."

He left all the appropriate doors standing open, and told the guards to stand within the room while Telemakos was on his own.

Telemakos went into the antechamber and cautiously scrubbed the grime from his face, astonished to discover how filthy he was. Athena grabbed hold of one of the towels and threw it in the basin. It landed with a splash, and she reached for another.

"Behave yourself, or they will send you away," Telemakos whispered to his sister, trying to restore the small space to a fit state. "Come, I must take this drink they've left me."

Telemakos backed out to the reception room again, nodded to the soldiers there, and stepped through to Abreha's study. It smelled delicious; the simmering wine was laced with clove and orange. Cup and knife and plate were laid out on the writing table. This must be how Socrates felt, Telemakos thought, expected to prepare his own execution.

"Open box," Athena said.

"Shh," he told her. "I don't need your instructions."

"Table box," she said. "Open najashi's table."

Telemakos stared at her. She knew this place, though Telemakos did not. She played in Abreha's office for an hour every morning.

"Najashi's box," Athena repeated impatiently, and reached forward to smack the low tabletop with her slim brown hand. "Open box."

Telemakos bent to look closely at the lacquered ebony. The marquetry panel in the center of the table formed a lid over a hidden well, like a large writing case. Telemakos moved the dishes aside.

"How does it work, Tena?" he whispered, aware of the soldiers standing guard in the outer room. "How did the najashi open it?"

She scrabbled her slender fingers lightly along the table's edge. She knew what she was looking for, but perhaps it was by accident that she found it. The panel sprang free of the worktop.

"Open box," Athena said with satisfaction. "See Boy's animals."

Inside, on top of a sheaf of neatly sorted documents, lay those finished maps Telemakos had sketched from the decaying wax the Star Master called the Plague Tablets.

Telemakos picked up the first sheet. It was his own drawing, the one with the ink-spattered pelicans that seemed to fly through a rainstorm across the top of the page. Someone else had written on it since then. The nameless coves and bays had been labeled. It had become a map of Hanish al-Kabir, Gebre Meskal's prison island. Telemakos had not recognized it by itself, separated from its archipelago, its outline grossly distorted by the untrained hand that made the wax sketch.

Telemakos narrowed his eyes and knelt studying the drawing like a puzzle, until Athena began to squirm and grab for the papyrus sheet.

"Tena's. Tena's animals."

"These aren't animals," Telemakos whispered. "Shh. Be quiet and I'll tell you. Do you see these chevrons? These are Gebre Meskal's guardian ships. These crosses are the najashi's men, soldiers, hiding in the back bays of al-Kabir."

The plans were crisscrossed with scratchings-out and scrawled notes. *No landing here*, said one, and another simply, *Dry*. It seemed clear to Telemakos what they meant. Abreha wanted to place an ambush around the prison but could not find any place to put his men ashore, or a water supply for them.

"Boats," Athena said, diving toward the map that lay beneath the one Telemakos held. "More boats."

"Those . . ." He studied the notes scrawled on this one, and managed to keep his voice low. "Those are Gebre Meskal's boats, but some of them have got the najashi's soldiers in them. . . ."

Suddenly he realized what the Plague Tablets were. The

crumbling, crude sketches he had been copying were Abreha's only maps of the Hanish Archipelago. The najashi had made them while he was in his self-imposed exile there, with an eye to invading the islands as soon as he and his men were able.

Telemakos was aghast to think how diligently he had been hurrying this project along. Numb with disbelief, he moved the maps aside and reached for the wad of palm and parchment that lay below them.

Abreha stood like a statue in the door to his study. Telemakos looked up. He did not know how long the najashi had been watching him. Telemakos suddenly became aware that his own face was frozen in a blistering glare of discovery and accusation: his lips were pressed together in a thin line, his nostrils pinched, one eyebrow cocked in concentration. His expression must radiate suspicion. Telemakos let his mouth go slack and opened his eyes wide.

"Two boats," Athena told the najashi. "Boy's animals, Tena's animals, Boy's boats."

"Why are you searching my desk?" Abreha asked quietly.

"Athena knew the maps were here," Telemakos said. "She wanted to see the animal pictures."

Abreha stood frowning, gazing down at the children. Telemakos could hear Tharan and Gedar talking in the next room, and for a heartbeat he thought Abreha was going to overlook the intrusion. Then Telemakos glanced down at the folded pages he still held.

They were letters, addressed to him. Most of them bore

Goewin's dragon seal. One bore his father's small, fine, careful script. Telemakos stared at the najashi.

"Put everything away," Abreha said.

Telemakos brandished the sheaf of stolen letters like a fire-brand.

"These are *mine!*"

"Put them away," said Abreha patiently.

Now Tharan came up behind the najashi and said, "You would be wise to search him."

"I don't take *other people's things,*" Telemakos said hotly.

His anger startled Athena.

"Boy?" she asked uncertainly, looking for quick reassurance.

Telemakos put down the letters and ran his fingers lightly over her hair. Abreha Anbessa said levelly to his lieutenant, "Take the baby up to Muna. I'll question the boy myself."

Athena was not prepared to accept this reasonably. She was tired, she was hungry, she had not seen Telemakos all day, and she did not like Tharan. She lowered her coppery eyebrows in a foreboding grimace.

"Put him away," she said with determination as Tharan stepped forward.

Still cradling her protectively, Telemakos whispered, "Little owlet, Tharan is going to take you for your supper—"

She let out a wail and pulled on Telemakos's hair with both hands, clinging to him with all her strength.

"Come on, Tena—"

Gedar and an attendant carrying a wine jar stood in the doorway, curious.

The najashi stepped behind Telemakos and took hold of him by his right wrist and the stump of his left shoulder, gently easing his arm away from Athena. Telemakos stiffened. This was somehow invasive, too intimate; the near destruction of his body was a private thing. Athena began to scream blue murder as Tharan unbuckled the straps of her harness, while Abreha held Telemakos still with his hand on the smooth ball of Telemakos's shoulder, controlling and lightly threatening. Telemakos did not dare struggle against his guardian. Only when Tharan pulled Athena away did Telemakos cry out softly, "Let me go! Let me take her up, or stop her screaming, so she'll go with you quietly, only—"

The najashi made no answer. He steered Telemakos around so that he was not able to see Tharan leave with the baby. Telemakos could hear the vizier begin to offer some explanation to Gedar before Tharan closed the door upon them.

Abreha pushed Telemakos down to sit on the floor and settled himself cross-legged before him. Then with one hand the najashi took firm hold of Telemakos again, pressing his fingertips against the inside of Telemakos's wrist; his other hand he slipped inside Telemakos's shirt, so that his palm lay against Telemakos's scarred chest, just over his heart.

"Now tell me, you young fox," Abreha said, "tell me truth-fully, the answer to a question that has been troubling me for a season and more. What made your grandfather so suddenly decide to send you here? Why are you in Himyar?"

Telemakos's heart lurched. He could feel the pulse in his wrist racing beneath Abreha's fingertips.

"Why are you in Himyar?"

Telemakos thought, He will know if I lie to him. He will know.

"Why are you in Himyar?"

"A slew of ugly threats were aimed at our house, just after the quarantine was lifted," Telemakos said. "My parents, my mother especially, were afraid to keep us there."

"What kind of threats?"

"They did not tell me." Telemakos chose his words with care. "They didn't want to frighten me."

Abreha sighed.

"Do you understand why I am angry, when it looks as though you are sorting through my private papers?"

"Those are *mine*," Telemakos retorted. "Why are you keep-ing them from me?"

"I live with the same fear that made your grandfather send you away. A great struggle for power and wealth goes on at all times over your head, and you are safer knowing nothing about it."

Telemakos made no answer, feeling his heartbeat beneath Abreha's hand and fingers. What in the world have they been trying to tell me in all those letters? What does Abreha know that I don't?

"Now tell me another thing," Abreha said. "What intrigue do you suspect concerning the Hanish Islands?"

Telemakos's heart was in his throat again, choking him.

"I know nothing of such an intrigue."

"Strictly speaking, that may be true," said Abreha. "But just now I heard you shrewdly hazarding that there is one, and I find it disturbing that so innocent a guest should leap to such conclusions."

Telemakos tried to keep his voice level.

"I've been put to work making copies of your maps. No one has told me anything about why they are so important, or so secret. What would anyone think, seeing these diagrams, but that you want the Hanish Islands under your control?"

"Will you keep your suspicions to yourself, or sow them abroad? Will you send a copy of your own map back to your map-loving aunt, the British ambassador, a riddle for the Sphinx to solve?"

"My aunt?" Telemakos whispered. "What is it to do with her?"

He was sure the unsteady beat of his own blood would betray her. Abreha could tell what Telemakos knew or did not know, or at the least cared about, by touching him lightly with his fingertips. Telemakos held silent, not trusting himself to speak.

But the najashi brushed the question by. He said irrelevantly,

"That lion has left his scent on you." Abreha withdrew the hand that had been held over Telemakos's heart to pluck straw from his hair, and tapped his cheek with it. "You might have asked someone to comb this out before you came down. You must have been back in Ghumdan at least an hour before the rest of us."

"I stayed with Menelik until—"

Telemakos stopped himself short, staring mesmerized at Abreha's fingers around his wrist.

"Until?" the najashi prompted in a voice like steel needles.

Telemakos tried to pull away from him then, in foolhardy, unguarded desperation.

"Until I came into the kennels?" Abreha guessed.

Oh, Telemakos lashed himself in fear and fury, what is the matter with me? I did not spill my secrets to Anako like this, when he was making Hara pull my fingernails out!

"What did you hear?"

Telemakos shuddered.

"Tell me what you heard."

Telemakos fell back on his boldest and most desperate ruse, the headlong assault. He whispered, "You spoke to Gedar. You are hunting an informer, someone who betrayed you to Gebre Meskal during the plague quarantine, which you had found a way around so that your trade with Aksum might continue without the emperor's sanction. Gedar discovered my grandfather to be the emperor's agent, and so sent threats to our house, not expecting those threats to drive me and my sister here."

Telemakos paused. His words sounded somehow sharp and calculating in his own ears, and he added, trying to simulate fearful innocence, "Will you use us as hostages, then, against my grandfather?"

"You are only hostage to your knowledge," Abreha answered, his voice calm. "Keep my secrets, and you are safe. Your grandfather is not the man we seek."

"Keep your secrets! Keep secret that you brought plague into your kingdom, and into Aksum!"

"You rail as though my intent was evil."

"You brought about the destruction of Deire!" Telemakos cried out.

"My people and I decided to suffer together," Abreha said seriously. "The question of quarantine was put to the Federation, and all were against it. The citizens of your ruined city Deire were not given any choice, when they were bound in their sickness within their walls by Gebre Meskal's soldiers."

Abreha's fingers were lax around Telemakos's wrist now, but kept steady on the beating vein.

I am dead if he discovers me, Telemakos thought. I am dead. He killed Hara just to please the emperor, and Hara was his own servant. I am nothing to him. I cut short all his venture in Aksum for two years. I am his enemy.

"My—my najashi—" Telemakos stammered. "My najashi, what surety do you need to trust me with your secrets?"

"Do you know the usual penalty for treason?"

"Yes," Telemakos whispered. "But . . ."

He hesitated because his understanding of loyalty, which seemed straightforward in his mind, might sound insolent on his tongue. The pulse in his wrist leapt and hammered.

"Go on," said Abreha softly.

"I am not yet sworn to serve you," Telemakos whispered, "so I cannot be guilty of treason."

There lay between them a long moment of frozen quiet. Then Abreha slipped his fingers from Telemakos's wrist down into his hand, pinching it open between them with his thumb in Telemakos's palm and his index finger piercing its back. Telemakos clenched his teeth: it felt as though Abreha were trying to make finger and thumb meet between the bones of his hand.

"Here is my plan for you, son of Medraut," Abreha said with cool resignation. "You were invited into this room; indeed, you were given leave to roam my palace freely, under a certain level of trust already, which you surely have wit enough to appreciate. You have betrayed that trust twice in a single evening. In punishment you shall not leave the scriptorium for the next season, nor have any consort with my Royal Scions during that time. And to ensure you do not try your fortune again in another such endeavor, I am going to fit you with an alarm, like a cat that must be kept away from one's pet songbirds. We shall bind on you a bracelet of ringing charms that will warn us of your coming. And—"

Abreha's calm voice never changed pitch.

"—And, beloved Morningstar, if I find you searching my desk again, or anyone else's, or if you are caught eavesdropping in my court—or if in any other way you seem likely to betray my affairs to my cousin the Aksumite emperor Gebre Meskal—I will have you crucified for a spy."

He let go of Telemakos's hand.

Telemakos stared down at his palm: it was marked with a white crescent where Abreha's thumbnail had bitten into it.

Let the najashi hang you up in my place next, you unholy creeping mongrel spy.

"Acknowledge me," Abreha said coldly.

Telemakos knelt before his guardian with his face pressed against the smooth pile of the silk carpet, as if he could hide himself that way. He closed his eyes. It was easy.

"My merciful najashi," Telemakos whispered. "I beg your forgiveness."

"Why should I forgive you?"

Telemakos did not dare raise his head. "May I speak boldly?"

"Speak then, Lij Telemakos."

It was a relief to hear his own name, even his own title. Telemakos turned his face aside so that his voice was not muffled by the carpet. The corner of his mouth brushed against the silk wool when he moved his lips. But he could muster no voice louder than a harsh whisper.

"The emperor Gebre Meskal has a favorite story." It was one of those Goewin had repeated to Telemakos, to distract him, as he had lain half-dead of blood poisoning and fever. "It tells of Menelik, the queen of Sheba's son, of his visit to Solomon, his father. When Menelik returns to his mother, he steals the Ark of the Covenant from Solomon. And Solomon discovers him. But instead of punishing him, Solomon gives him the Ark and lets him go free."

Telemakos stopped speaking for a moment, and Abreha waited in dangerous silence.

"Solomon is remembered for his wisdom," Telemakos whispered into the carpet. "But when I see Solomon's portrait in the old pictures, I am not struck by his wisdom. I see forgiveness in his face."

Now he dared raise his head.

"I remember your truce with Gebre Meskal," Telemakos whispered. "I was there. You wore the look of Solomon, the face of forgiveness."

Abreha did not answer. Telemakos swallowed, wondering if he had gone too far. He heard Abreha move to his desk, and heard the crackle of parchment and the soft, soft splash of a brush moving quickly over a page.

Abreha blew the ink dry and folded the sheet.

"'Of the tree of the knowledge of good and evil you shall not eat,'" the najashi said, "'for in the day you eat of it you shall die.'"

There was the slick squeal of steel against silver as Abreha drew his dagger. Telemakos knelt tense but unflinching, head down, as Abreha parted the hair at his neck. The dagger's blade brushed cold against Telemakos's skin, but all the najashi did was to shave off one of the matted elflocks at the base of Telemakos's skull.

"Raise your head," Abreha commanded him. "Watch."

The najashi pierced the tip of his dagger through all the thicknesses of the folded page he had been writing on. Then he twined the shorn hank of Telemakos's hair into a rough silver filament, and threaded it through the holes in the sheet. Finally he twisted the great signet ring from his finger. He placed it on his open palm, held flat before him where Telemakos could see it.

"There is no solid thing, no object of value, that I would not forgive you," Abreha said quietly. "Not Solomon's Ark, if I had it; not even Solomon's ring, which I hold in my hand. There is no tangible thing you could take from me that I would not forgive you. But I will not forgive you stolen knowledge."

He lit a stick of wax and sealed the writing with his mark, with Telemakos's hair fixed through the seal, so that even if the seal were to be prised off unbroken, the folds of the page could not be opened without the hair being cut as well.

"In the hands of your enemy, this is warrant for your execution."

God help me, this cannot be happening, Telemakos thought.

"But let us keep it safe in the hands of your friend," Abreha added, and tucked the sealed page into his sash. "So long as I hold this on my person, your life is secure. Let me help you up, Telemakos."

He raised Telemakos to his feet at last, and stood with his hands on his ward's shoulders. Telemakos kept his head down, not risking the insolence of meeting the najashi's gaze.

Abreha kissed him lightly on the side of his face.

"That is how the Romans seal a covenant," the najashi said. "Guard my knowledge, and I shall guard your life. I still expect your pledge of service to be made to me someday."

He drove Telemakos gently toward the door. "Compose yourself. You are dining with my guest tonight. Gedar need not know what has passed between us."

He let Telemakos go.

Later, alone in the small, high room where he worked and slept, Telemakos knelt by the dark eastern window with his head resting along his forearm, staring out over glittering San'a. The colored windows of the tower city gleamed like eyes and fireflies. Athena was sobbing below him in the nursery. He was not allowed to see her. They had set a guard by his door. The baby's sobs sounded breathless and pathetic, as though she had been screaming hysterically for a long time and no longer had the energy to keep herself going. Telemakos knew no one would ever get her to eat anything that night.

He chewed at his knuckles and tried to think.

What is Goewin telling me? What is in those letters that

is so revealing, so secret, so damning that the Lion Hunter of Himyar will not let me see them?

Perhaps it is something to do with the appointment of a new British ambassador to Himyar. Maybe Gwalchmei was really dismissed for some disgrace Abreha does not think I should know about, and Goewin does. Or did Gwalchmei, like me, know something he shouldn't?

Telemakos stared at the city lights and gnawed at the back of his single fist until he fell asleep, and fell drowning into another dream.

He swam beneath a deep green salt sea with his hands bound behind his back, at such a distance from air and light that his body seemed twice its normal weight. He despaired of ever fighting to the surface before his lungs filled with heavy water and dragged him into the cold dark that plunged endlessly away below him. He kicked frantically upward, chest exploding and throat afire, toward a gold star of shimmering brightness far above. Then suddenly Telemakos broke through to warmth and wind and sunlight. He drew greedy breaths of sweet, clean air, relief flooding his veins. He shook the water from his eyes and looked about him.

The sea stretched endlessly away on every side. He could see nothing in any direction: no land, no sail, no raft, no drifting branch. He did not know where he was. The horizon was limitless; the sun stood overhead and told him nothing. He could not swim—his hands were still bound. He was alone.

Desolation so choked him that Telemakos began to cry in his sleep.

That woke him. He was cramped and cold, still sitting with his head against the windowsill.

He dragged cushions and his coverlet over to the pulley hole in the corner and made his bed on the floor there, with his head close to the shaft that led to the nursery. He could hear Athena below him breathing gustily in her sleep; the warm air of the room beneath filtered up to him. It smelled of sandalwood.

To be continued in THE EMPTY KINGDOM

AUTHOR'S NOTE

There is an Ethiopian proverb that goes, "To lie about a far country is easy." The world of Telemakos's adolescence is a world that exists mostly in my head, though parts of it bear passing resemblances to ancient places in the world we know. My maps are imperfect. Too often, when I can't find an accurate record of something, I make it up.

The river at Mai Barea does not exist; probably it never did exist. I don't know what language the street children of al-Muza spoke, or if anyone has ever been mad enough to try to teach a lion to hunt like a dog. "Sheba" is more correctly "Saba." I am constantly running into questions of detail, accuracy, and consistency that would strangle me if I did not make up a reasonable standard answer for myself. Would a South Arabian king eat a red-legged partridge or would he consider it unclean? How much do you have to refine olive oil before you can burn it as a light? Where does basil come from *originally*? (Vanilla is mentioned as a flavoring in *The Winter Prince*, but I have since discovered that it is native to Central America.) Could you really recover from a case of blood poisoning as dire as Telemakos's without the assistance of antibiotics?

Consider Medraut as a physician. He speaks of plague as though he understands immunity. This is a concept that did not exist until very recently, though there is evidence that there may have been some understanding of it in ancient times. Medraut uses opium as a painkiller and a sedative; it's unlikely it was used as either in the sixth century, nor was it considered addictive. There was no concept of addiction as an evil then as there is today, and anesthesia is a product of the nineteenth century. But it seems right for Medraut to think as he does about illness and healing, because he is an innovative physician and because, like his mother, he sometimes uses medicine as a weapon. He and those close to him are well aware that his skill is a double edged blade, and also that he stands outside societal norms in many ways.

I love using detail, physical detail, to make my stories seem real. I love naming specific birds and spices and fabrics, both familiar and exotic; I think this detail gives my stories (or anyone's) *verisimilitude*. I do my best to make these details accurate to the time and place I am writing about, but I cannot guarantee their accuracy. Is *Le Morte D'Arthur* an accurate portrayal of King Arthur's court? It postdates the historical Arthur by a thousand years. I do not like to draw attention to my own inaccuracies, but I know they exist. This is a work of fiction. Enjoy these lies about a far country, and if you can, forgive them.

Elizabeth E. Wein
Perth, Scotland
February 2007

Glossary

(G=Ge'ez, or ancient Ethiopic; A=Amharic, or modern Ethiopian; SA=Sabaean, or ancient South Arabian; MA=modern Arabian)

Amole (A): Block of cut salt used as currency.

Anbessa (G, A): Lion.

Bitwoded (A): Literally, "Beloved"; a bestowed, and unusual, noble title.

Emebet (A): Title for a young princess.

Hawri (MA): A narrow, open fishing boat, like a canoe.

Injera (A): Flat bread made from tef, Ethiopian grain.

Kat (MA): A mild stimulant in use throughout the Horn of Africa and the Arabian Peninsula. It grows as a small bush and the leaves are chewed fresh.

Kolo (A): Fried barley (eaten as a snack).

Lij (A): Title for a young prince (similar to European "childe").

Meskal (G, A): Feast of the Cross (literally "cross"), religious holiday taking place at the end of September.

Mukarrib (SA): Federator.

Najashi (SA): King.

Nebir (A): Leopard.

Ras (A): Title for a duke or prince.

Shamma (A): Cotton shawl worn over clothes by men and women.

Suq (MA): Market.

Tef (A): Ethiopian grain.

Wadi (MA): A valley, carved by rainwater runoff, which remains dry except in the rainy season.

Woyzaro (A): Title for a lady or princess.

NOTE: The Ethiopian new year falls on 11 September in the Western calendar.

FAMILY TREE (Abreha)

Mikael (insane;
sequestered
at Debra Damo)

Woyzaro
(Princess)
Makeda

Hector (killed
in war between
Aksum and Himyar)

PRIAMOS
(Aksumite ambassador
to Britain)

Ityopis
(councilor to
Gebre Meskal)

ABREHA ANBESSA, najashi
(king) of Himyar and mukarrib
(federator) of South Arabia

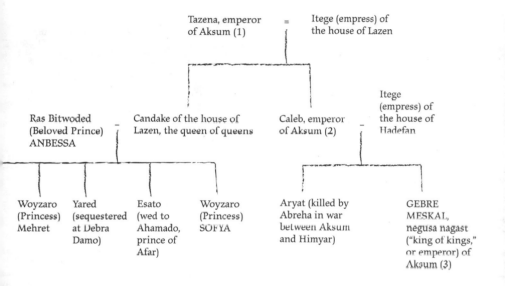

Tazena, emperor of Aksum (1) = Itege (empress) of the house of Lazen

Ras Bitwoded (Beloved Prince) ANBESSA — Candake of the house of Lazen, the queen of queens

Caleb, emperor of Aksum (2) — Itege (empress) of the house of Hadefan

Woyzaro (Princess) Mehret

Yared (sequestered at Debra Damo)

Esato (wed to Ahamado, prince of Afar)

Woyzaro (Princess) SOFYA

Aryat (killed by Abreha in war between Aksum and Himyar)

GEBRE MESKAL, negusa nagast ("king of kings," or emperor) of Aksum (3)

People with names in UPPER CASE letters appear in this book

FAMILY TREE (Telemakos)

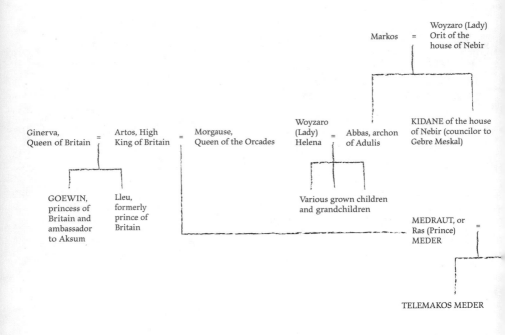

Markos = Woyzaro (Lady)
Orit of the
house of Nebir

Ginerva,
Queen of Britain = Artos, High
King of Britain = Morgause,
Queen of the Orcades

Woyzaro
(Lady) = Abbas, archon
Helena of Adulis

KIDANE of the house
of Nebir (councilor to
Gebre Meskal)

GOEWIN,
princess of
Britain and
ambassador
to Aksum

Lleu,
formerly
prince of
Britain

Various grown children
and grandchildren

MEDRAUT, or
Ras (Prince) =
MEDER

TELEMAKOS MEDER

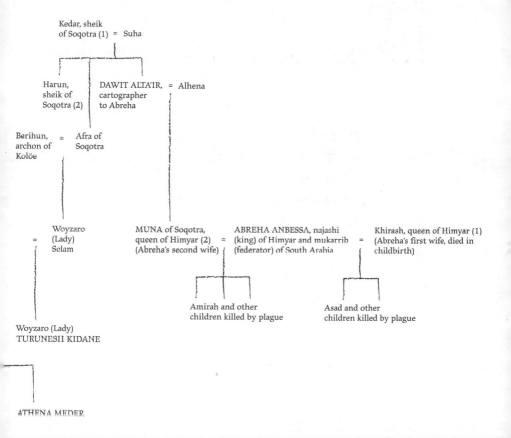

Kedar, sheik
of Soqotra (1) = Suha

Harun,   DAWIT ALTA'IR, = Alhena
sheik of   cartographer
Soqotra (2)   to Abreha

Berihun, = Afra of
archon of   Soqotra
Kolöe

Woyzaro   MUNA of Soqotra,   ABREHA ANBESSA, najashi   Khirash, queen of Himyar (1)
= (Lady)   queen of Himyar (2) = (king) of Himyar and mukarrib = (Abreha's first wife, died in
Selam   (Abreha's second wife) (federator) of South Arabia   childbirth)

Amirah and other   Asad and other
children killed by plague   children killed by plague

Woyzaro (Lady)
TURUNESH KIDANE

ATHENA MEDER

People with names in UPPER CASE letters appear in this book

NOTE: the name of a "house" is carried through the female line. Telemakos
inherits his family name, Nebir, through his mother Turunesh, but she takes the
name from her father Kidane only because he has no sisters, and his wife, being
of Arabian descent, does not belong to an Aksumite noble house. Telemakos is
Kidane's heir, but if he has children they will be of their mother's house, not his. It
is Athena's children who will preserve the name of the house of Nebir.

Elizabeth E. Wein (pronounced WEEN) was born in New York City and grew up in England, Jamaica, and Pennsylvania. She has a B.A. from Yale and a Ph.D. from the University of Pennsylvania.

She has written three other novels in her ongoing Arthurian/Aksumite cycle: *The Winter Prince*, *A Coalition of Lions*, and *The Sunbird*. *The Empty Kingdom*—the second book of the sequence called The Mark of Solomon—is forthcoming.

Elizabeth Wein spent twenty-four years of her life as a student. She and her husband share a passion for maps, and they both fly small planes as private pilots. They live in Scotland with their two young children.

Visit her Web site at **www.elizabethwein.com**